DOUBLE EXPOSURE

DOUBLE EXPOSURE

BY GAIL HARPER

STORY LINE PRESS

1989

Published by Story Press, Inc.
d.b.a. Story Line Press
403 Continental Street
Santa Cruz, California
95060

First American Printing

Publication of this work is made possible in part by grants from the National Endowment for the Arts.

ISBN: 0-934257-26-4

Book design by Lysa McDowell
Cover photos by Paul Schraub

FOR GEORGE HITCHCOCK

PART ONE

PASADENA, CALIFORNIA
FEBRUARY 14, 1974

The day they released me, the air had that wonderful garbagy smell that is so L.A. I took it all in: car exhaust, sidewalk dirt, the smell of the winos by the bus benches. I had a good look at some hard-core city because my mom couldn't find the freeway entrance. We drove round and round. We passed a mirrored skyscraper three times. Mom cussed everything, including me. I rolled my window down all the way and let the wind stampede through the Chevy, carrying with it coded messages. Every smell told a story. My mother yelled, "Goddamn stinking city!"

When Darrell disappeared, I thought of all the cliffs, canyons, bodies of water, forests, freeways; I thought of bottles of pills, knives, guns, ropes; I thought of everything in the world he could turn against himself. I pictured him standing by a freeway somewhere, dressed in tired levis and a

Hawaiian shirt faded to an anemic yellow, his lank hair lifting and slapping across his forehead each time a car flew by, registering each failure. I see his thumb sinking to his side as his fatigue increases; standing quickly tires him because of his lousy posture. His chest is so caved in and his spine so mired in flesh that for him there is no such thing as support. He needs something to lean against, some retaining wall or overpass, or better yet a car seat to sink into. Nothing is available. Nobody stops for Darrell.

I see him again, kicking sand along a deserted beach at three in the morning, wearing a grey sweatshirt with a hood, monk-like, yet not like a monk; he has no grace. I see him wetting his tennis shoes in the surf, hoping for numbness? He is chilled, yes; but the climate here is so temperate that numbness is impossible. If he is looking for extremes he will have to create them himself.

Would Darrell take to the mountains? I couldn't see him negotiating the slopes on foot; he is more the kind of animal that drags itself to water and relies on buoyancy. The mountains are for nimbler creatures. Could he drag himself to a cliff's edge? I can see him winding along mountain roads in a car, finding a turn-off, a favorite vantage point of suburbanites on Sunday drives, slamming the door with finality, crunching over the graveled parking area to the edge. But I think he would hesitate there. Maybe he would weep. He would sit and look out over the city lights and the wind would bathe his face. No, he would not die that way. He does not want the final clumsiness of scrambling over rocks, the awkward fall; he wants a moment of graceful flight. An overdose then?

High school was something I'd almost forgotten about. I hoped they'd forgotten about me. I didn't have any use for college prep or home economics. But the month was October, and all the boys and girls were deep in school already, books up their butts. As soon as we sailed off the freeway, Mom had that old Chevy pointed in the direction of Asshole High. I got the idea pretty fast when we passed the apartment without even slowing down.

"Hey, where are you taking me?" I demanded.

"School," she said, lighting a cigarette. She wouldn't even look at me.

"I've had enough punishment. Can't I even change my clothes first?" I was a bit overdressed, wearing the same clothes I was busted in at the party two weeks previous.

"Doesn't matter," said Mom, exhaling.

We pulled up in front of the high school, and Mom jumped out of the car.

"Snap it up." she said.

I didn't even have a smoke to ease the interview. It was like going in naked. Except that I was wearing a dress made from an old tapestry, and scarlet tights to set it off. I'm sure I made an impression on the dildo whose job it was to welcome me back. He kept looking me up and down, up and down. I made a point of looking him up and down, too, but neither he or my mother took note. Mom quickly filled his little office with cigarette smoke. I watched the smoke hang over his head. I thought of razors and knives. All the time he talked about discipline and the value of education in a complex world. I would have liked to have taken Mother's cigarette and told him to bend over for easy insertion. But I kept my mouth shut. I was reformed.

A soft-bodied animal slumped on my bed. Darrell come to argue his case. He is hunched as though to protect his vulnerable stomach, but he looks soft all over; is his back as soft as his stomach? I have no desire to touch. He is listing all of the women he has wanted and never had. He describes them in order of his preference, telling how each one rejected him. All of them rejected him. I am fascinated by his mouth. I have never seen such a bitter mouth. It twists; it is ravaged; he has lost control of it. His tongue struggles against dryness. I want to offer him water, but I am afraid to interrupt his speech. I am far down his list, he says; I am not that important. He has a top ten. The eyes are the right color, he says, and the hair. He likes the cheek-bones. The build would be right except for the breasts. He wants bigger breasts. He runs his tongue ineffectually around the inside of his mouth. "I need a drink of water," he says at last.

I sat on one of those green benches where the paint was peeling so bad it stuck me in the butt no matter how I arranged it. I was having a hell of a time. It was lunch hour. My mother'd left me there just in time for the event. First thing I did upon leaving the principal's office was to go into one of the girl's johns that wasn't locked. They had ten johns, and all of them were locked except two. This was because the girls were constantly sneaking cigarettes in the john, and the folks in charge felt that this had to be stopped. Two women had been hired to watch over the kiddies during lunch hour, and somehow the folks in charge figured that two women couldn't control ten johns. So they locked eight of them. This made sense to them, but not to the people who had to piss, since there were only two stalls to a john and a whole mob of smokers who liked to hide in the stalls while they smoked. When the ladies came in to enforce the law, the smokers would drop their cigarettes in the pot and sit down fast. Meanwhile, the people who had to piss were just about busting their bladders trying to hold on. It was an ugly situation. I braved the mess so I could put on some make-up. It wasn't easy. Believe me, it was wall-to-wall bodies. Everybody sort of stiffened and looked toward the door when I opened it. This happened any time the door opened. Cigarettes disappeared behind backs like fish behind seaweed; everybody prepared to drop the evidence if it was Her. A little bit of smoke managed to crawl along the ceiling and slip out the door each time it opened, but the air was still pretty fogged over. There weren't any windows, just a small vent that opened to the outside of the building. The air was enough to kill the weak. Some girl bumped my elbow while I was putting on the old eyeliner and I sort of leaned over her and gave her a long look, sort of like the look those video things in banks and shops give you. You know, like "Try it, I'm getting it all down." I'm real tall, like six feet tall, and I can impress people easily. I impressed her. She took her cigarette over to another corner of the bathroom.

The air outside seemed fresh by comparison, but one look in the direction of the mountains was enough to confirm that the air was pretty damn thick. Asshole High is about five miles away from the foothills, and on most afternoons you can't see the mountains for the smog. When they do appear, like after a rain, it's like sighting a whale in the birdbath in your backyard. I mean it.

So I was sitting on the goddamn bench in my tapestry dress, trying not to snag my tights on the paint. I must have been some picture for those goons. I had real long hair then, down to my waist, and I painted my eyes up real dark, so they kind of made the rest of my face look insignificant, which is what I wanted. When I was feeling anti-social, which was ninety-five percent of the time, I let my hair hang down close to my face, sort of like a half-drawn curtain. Then I could sort of peer out at everybody and still feel protected. Like I said, I'm real tall, and most of my length is in my arms and legs, so when I spread out I'm hard to avoid. When I try to limit myself to a small area, I just look kind of folded in on myself; I look like one of those goddamn telephone repair trucks with all those cranes and ladders sticking out all over the place. And it's like I have an incomplete nervous system, like somehow the network didn't make it all the way down to my hands and feet, because I feel this lack of control. Or maybe it's lack of confidence. Anyway, the goons were really checking it out. A couple of guys were standing nearby, mashing sandwiches into their faces and staring. One of them caught my eye and then pointed at his leg. I figured he was making a slur on my red tights, so I looked around to see if any monitors were looking and then, seeing that all systems were go, I stood up, turned around, and as majestically as I could, I lifted my dress and stuck my butt out at them. Then I sat down again. The guys were holding their sandwiches in mid-air, waiting for some kind of aftershock, I suppose. When they got it under control again, they slipped into the crowd around the dining hall and didn't bother to come back. I sort of wanted a cigarette, but I didn't want to mess with the bathroom and I didn't want to violate any of the boundaries they'd set up. It wouldn't do to get caught smoking in the parking lot after just having been sprung from Juvie. So I forgot about the cigarette. I watched the goons. The surfer goons were the worst. I bet half of them never set foot on a surfboard. They just squeezed lemon juice on their hair to bleach it and squeezed Sea and Ski on the rest of themselves so they'd be brown, and then they wore white or baby-blue shirts to set off their tans, their blue eyes, and their big white teeth. All of those goons had big white teeth. I was starting to feel depressed.

Darrell's uncomprehending eyes confront me. He wants to tell me a story. It has everything to do with his frustration but nothing to do with me. I sit on my desk and thump my heels against wood; Darrell has almost forgotten me in the telling, only notices me when my attention begins to wander. He has a top ten list of girls he wants; I don't even rank sixth, he says.

✴

I tried to stay reformed, but after three weeks of the same old shit my patience quit. Mom wasn't any better; she went to work and came home in the evenings and started in on the drinking, and I'd sit in my bedroom and try to read or something and I'd go crazy with the sound of the TV and Mom crying and the neighbors fighting. I'd give up on whatever I was trying to do and go sit on my Mom's Chevy in her parking stall in the back of the building and smoke a joint in the dark and listen to everybody's TVs chattering. Sometimes I'd watch the windows in the back of the apartment house to see if anybody would pass by or maybe look out, but the windows were so high and narrow I never could see much more than somebody's head going by, and nobody looked out because there was nothing to look at except identical windows in the back of other apartment houses or the parking stalls, and nothing much ever happened in the parking stalls. Since it was November the evenings were pretty cool out, and most people stayed indoors. So I had the stalls all to myself, and I sat out there all bundled up and hated the thought of going back inside. But when I was stoned enough and cold enough I'd go back and help Mom to bed if she was passed out, and then I'd go to bed myself, and the dope would help me sleep. Then in the morning if it was a weekday I'd get up with Mom and we'd get dressed and eat without talking to each other, except sometimes she'd look funny at my clothes. She'd drop me off at school on her way to work, and even kiss me on the cheek sometimes if she wasn't in a real foul mood, and I'd walk down the hall rubbing lipstick off my face. I'd walk down the hall until I came to the other side of the school, and then I'd break my first rule of the day. I'd walk off campus and walk a little ways into the residential area, and then I'd light up a joint and keep walking until I'd finished it, and then I'd get back on campus in plenty of time for class. Rule number one: Once on campus you don't set foot off campus until the final bell rings at 3:00 p.m. I sat in the back of the room during all of my classes and I never said anything if I could help it, and I watched all the goons go through their motions. When lunchtime rolled around, I'd sneak off campus again and smoke another joint, but I had to be extra careful then because the cops were always cruising those streets looking for truants, and it was hard to get on and off campus without bumping into a security guard. Years of playing cowboys and Indians paid off there; I was real good at sneaking around and I never got caught. I'd sneak back on campus in time to buy some junk for lunch and watch the goons some more, and then I'd go spacing off to PE class and put on those goddamn smelly gym clothes that I never washed, and I'd fake whatever it was the teacher wanted us to do for the day. Or if it was something I absolutely refused to do, like swimming, I'd stay in my street clothes and hang around with the other fuckoffs and the medical excuses and I'd take an F for the day. After PE I'd drag off to my afternoon classes and hide in the back of the room again and draw pictures or try to get some sleep, and then three o'clock would roll around and I'd get out of there as fast as I could. Usually I'd walk downtown after school and have a bite to eat somewhere, and then I'd wander around and watch the shoppers. When I was in the mood I'd do some shopping myself, ripping off a little something here and there. I'd just act like I knew what I was doing and walk off with two or three layers of clothing on and a few goodies in my bag, and they'd tell me to come back again. I spent three weeks like that and then I decided I wanted to see something else.

When he finally allowed me to speak, I intended to be delicate but honest. He had asked if I found him repulsive. How could I say what he was to me without injuring him? He had beautiful coloring, true; but it was the beauty of an exotic insect that wears a veneer of startling color in contrast to what otherwise is a totally grotesque body. He was a specimen for National Geographic, not a potential bedmate. Yet he was sitting on my bed, asking me to donate my body to his experiment. "No," I said. "No, you are not repulsive . . . ."

The guy I talked to was the same dildo who had welcomed me back. He didn't act very friendly after I told him what I wanted. He fingered his tie and shuffled some papers on his desk and told me that the school's policy was not to graduate people early unless they proved exceptional in ability and ambition. I told him that I was real exceptional and ambitious, too, or I wouldn't want to get out so bad. He said that wasn't what he meant, and he started to explain that you had to be already admitted to some hotshot college for the Spring semester or something, and I could see that I wasn't going to get anywhere with this guy, so I hunted around in my purse while he went on and I pulled out a cigarette and lit up. He stopped talking and looked at me for a minute, and then he blew his cool and grabbed my wrist and took the cigarette out of my hand. "Give me the rest of those," he said, and I told him he could go out and buy his own. He suspended me, of course, and while I was out I decided never to go back.

2.

I did a little research the day after the Big Dump and found out that since I was just over eighteen years of age I couldn't legally be made to stay in high school. Plus I discovered that I could enter the local junior college and make up my high school credits while working toward a college degree. I wrote all this down in a note to my mom and left it on the counter in the kitchenette with the notice of my suspension from high school, and then I went out job-hunting. I applied in all the local shops for a job as a salesgirl, and the way I lied about my experience you would have thought I'd been a floor manager at Saks Fifth Avenue at one time. Things looked real promising. I went back to the apartment that evening with mixed feelings. I felt good because I was out of school and I was going to make some money, but I felt nervous because I knew Mom was going to be royally pissed off when I got back, in spite of my tactful note. She was waiting for me at the door, bottle in hand, her face all knotted up and ready for a crying jag.

"Now Mom," I said, "Did you read my note?" I was very diplomatic about the whole thing.

She started blubbering "Goddamn your note, goddamn your note . . . ."

She was pretty far gone, and she let me lead her over to the couch and sit down beside her, and I explained to her that everything was going to be all right and that I was going to graduate from high school, just a little later than usual, and that I was even going to go to college like she never did. And I asked her if I'd been any trouble since I'd been back from Juvie. She just cried and didn't say anything, which meant that I was right. I told her that I'd been out job-hunting all afternoon and I was going to make some money somewhere at a regular sort of job, just like she was doing. I tried to pat her on the back, but she pushed my hand away and muttered something like, "I'll believe it when I see it," which sort of pissed me off, but I stayed cool and said that I was going to fix myself some dinner. I went behind the counter and started fixing a sandwich, watching Mom all the while. She wouldn't look at me; she just held on to her bottle and cried.

Has anyone seen Darrell Schleyer? He slouches through my dreams at night; he makes irregular appearances. Has anyone seen Darrell Schleyer? He followed me whenever he saw me passing by; that's how bad it got to be. I didn't know what to do with him. I had made the mistake of being friendly to the local pariah. I don't make such distinctions according to other people's rules, but he apparently did; I guess he was grateful for the attention. It was a novelty that ballooned into an obsession. So the lumbering lump followed me with a docility that was a wonder to behold. Always, "How are you?" offered up as if it were a proposal of something more, some evening's entertainment, or maybe a longer engagement. . . emotion trembling in his slack face as he asked. I wanted to scream at him, "I'm fine, I'm always fine, can't you see?" but I mumbled a greeting instead and walked by with my face nearly averted. I couldn't help seeing his eyes, moist with some passion, a despairing insistence? I should have stopped then and explained. How does one explain to a person so painfully alone that he will have to stay where he was placed? Not without an explosion. Where is Darrell Schleyer?

The first job I got was driving this vegetable around and being a companion to him. I had to have a car, and Mom came through with a late-fifties Oldsmobile. I loaded and unloaded the vegetable, drove him to his special school, and cruised the town with him, always talking to him about anything I could think of, just like his mom told me to. He was about fifteen years old and shapeless. When he wasn't sitting in the car with me, he sat in a wheelchair. He never said anything, and I wasn't sure about how much he could hear. His mom was nervous and fluttery. She talked to him very rapidly, always telling him to be good and to be nice to me. He acted like she didn't exist. She would pat him and arrange him, and he would settle back into his blob shape without visibly moving. I was uncomfortable with him at first, and tried to be careful about what I said in case he ever decided to relate anything to his mom, but after a few days I realized that he just didn't relate at all. Zero. So I started to say the most outrageous things I could think of. I'd say, "Wouldn't you like to go fuck Mom with a three-foot dildo?" He wouldn't flinch. When I got bored with that game, I started picking up hitchhikers and introducing the vegetable to them as my brother. I would be very serious and explain how my brother had been in a terrible accident or a fight or something, and the hitchhiker would be very sympathetic. Lucky for me I didn't have a hitchhiker with me the time I crashed the car. I'd just picked the kid up at his special school in San Marino and was taking the scenic route back to his mother's house, I hadn't even worked up something to bend his ear with, when this idiot poodle ran out in front of my car. I swerved to miss it, and before I knew what was happening the car bucked up and over the curb and smashed into a tree. I went face first into the windshield. It didn't knock me out, just stunned me, and I sat for a minute fingering my face to see if anything was busted; my chin was all bloody, but everything else seemed to be okay. Then I flashed on the vegetable. I eased myself around to have a looksee, and I saw him rolled up in a blob on the floor in the back. I leaned over the seat and was poking him to see if he was okay when I heard a man saying, "Miss . . ." I sat up and looked out the window, and a cop was standing there on the lawn with the lady who owned the lawn. The cop opened the car door and asked if I was okay, and I asked him to check the vegetable. The vegetable seemed a little paler than usual, but other than that he was fine. The cop put us both in his squad car and took us to the hospital where they sewed my chin up and determined that the vegetable wasn't any more in shock than he usually was. Then they called his mom, who became hysterical immediately. That was the end of my first job, and I didn't ask the lady for any recommendations.

When I felt that hand on my arm, I knew it was Darrell. Nobody had hands like his, so tentative yet demanding. No

one else would have stopped me like that, a restraining hand and then those eyes accusing me: you betrayed me, they said. You made me feel special, and then you let me be ordinary again. I had a rarefied moment; I felt a focusing of desire; I was lifted from undefined need. Give me definition. Obscurity is worse than death.

I couldn't define anything for you, Darrell.

✳

I was on the hunt for my second job when my brother materialized with a friend. My brother told me that he and his friend Gary had set up a ceramics studio in a storefront. I abandoned the job hunt for a while and went along with them to see the studio. I hadn't seen my brother in a couple of months, but he didn't have much to say except that he was real excited about getting into ceramics. I noticed that he looked skinnier and figured that he'd been doing some speed. He was pretty much the same old Dan, chainsmoking and not saying much. He drove us to his studio in his Mercury. I felt pretty good, seeing him again. It was real sunny and warm out, one of those freak December days in Southern Cal, and we had all the windows down, and we were smoking a joint, letting the wind suck the fumes away. The three of us were in the front seat, me in the middle with my knees up around my chin, and I kept stealing glances at my brother. He has long, big bones like me, and he had his arm resting on the door, and the wind was ruffling the blond hair on his arm. I could see he'd been out in the sun because he had freckles all down his arms and on his face. He looked good. But then so did his friend.

Darrell Schleyer sitting on a bench under a tree by one of the mirror pools, the sun splotchy on his face, confronting me.

Darrell Schleyer with his windbreaker unzipped and flapping as he talks angrily, his mouth so dry that all I can think of is water. The sunlight swarming on the water in the mirror pool. One of my acquaintances is sailing a paper boat on the water fifty yards away. I find myself leaning toward him, my acquaintance, away from Darrell who suddenly catches my arm.

The first time me and Gary made it was at his mother's house on his little bed in the afternoon. His mom was at work and his sister was still at school. He seemed to know when both of them would be back, so he wasn't nervous at all. He knocked around in his closet and brought out his stash, rolled us a joint, and we sat on his unmade bed and smoked. I liked the way he did everything without wasting any time or energy. I hadn't stopped feeling tall and clumsy around him, and as we smoked I wondered more and more what he thought about me. He never said much. I wondered if I was just going to be another one of his buddies. I was really gone thinking about this when I felt the bed moving, and I looked at him. He was lying down on his back, all stretched out. He looked me right in the eye and said, "Why don't you lie down, too, and then we can both look up at the sky through the window." I didn't say anything; I just did what he suggested. I felt like a goddamn virgin. When I was lying next to him, I felt all light-headed and strange. He didn't do anything for a while, and I tried to concentrate on the sky, which was very blue. I was about to say that I was getting too dizzy watching the sky like that when I felt his hand slip up under my blouse, and he was suddenly kissing me. So we weren't going to be buddies. I tried to get into what he was doing, but I felt like I was at one of those formal dinner parties where you've got about ten pieces of silverware to use and you don't know which one to use for which course and you lose your appetite thinking about it.

I wish I could remember some of the names he told me. He listed off names when he was sitting on my bed and I was watching the sun light up dust particles in the air and trying not to look too closely at the corners of his mouth. My feelings were as random as those bits of dust wandering, and my fascination strayed as inevitably and stupidly as a moth toward Darrell's pain. If I'd had any foresight I would have listened to the names and had a record of connections. I could have followed the names like tracks in sand or like stars in constellations. As it was I had nothing to follow, not even a direction to start in.

✴

I found a new job that was strictly up the butt. The only reason I took it was because I needed the money and I wanted to keep Mom off my back. The job involved store windows. I was on a crew that painted Christmas scenes in the windows of businesses all around the San Gabriel Valley for a fee. This was very seasonal stuff, and at first I thought it wouldn't be so bad because the job couldn't last beyond the Big Day. The bucks could have been big if we had moved fast enough, and if our boss hadn't been a crook. But goddamn we were slow, and the boss was the crook of the year. This guy was a real asshole. He had this cheap businessman image, always wore suits and drove a car that looked like a sawed-off hearse. When I walked into his office I was greeted by this secretary who looked like a bomb went off in her hair. There were a few guys sitting around. The boss came out of his private office and handed out little pieces of paper and asked us to demonstrate our artistic ability. Me and the guys sat and drew pictures of Santa Claus for the goon. He hardly even looked at our drawings, and he hired us all right away.

Then he took us out for a demonstration. He was going to show us how to do a good job fast so we could make lots of money and he could get his cut. He took us to the edge of the business district, to some rinky-dink insurance company which had an enormous picture window for a front wall. We waited on the sidewalk with our collars up while the boss went inside and said something to one of the secretaries, who nodded and smiled and glanced at us and then walked to the back of the room and knocked on a panelled wood door. A man in a business suit came out and our boss went up to him and shook his hand and sort of waved in our direction without looking around. We could see the man watching our boss talk. The man smiled and pulled out his wallet and handed a couple of bills to our boss. They shook hands again and the man went back behind his panelled door, and our boss turned around and came striding toward us, and all the secretaries looked up and smiled. The boss pushed open the heavy glass door and said, "Now let's get moving," as the door shut behind him. There was sort of a problem because there were all these plants in front of the window, but the boss didn't let that stop him. He took off his jacket, draped it over an azalea, and waded into the shrubs. He looked at the window and then twisted around, being surrounded by shrubs, and motioned for paints. "Red paint and a brush," he said. One of the guys handed him the stuff. The secretaries watched from their desks. "Now, use generous, quick brush strokes," he said, reaching as high as he could. He was wearing red socks. He swabbed some red circles on the glass. "Green, now." Some kids stopped to watch. "Make your leaves like this." He made some stabbing motions and produced something that was supposed to represent holly leaves. It didn't look so good. I was starting to feel sort of embarrassed. The secretaries had gone back to their typewriters, glancing up now and then. Our boss painted some more holly leaves and then showed us how to do a fast Santa. He dripped some paint on the window. "Damn. Got a rag?" I offered him a kleenex. "Well goddamn," he said, smearing the drip. The kids left. The guys kept shifting their weight and fiddling with their collars. The window looked pretty tacky. I was afraid the man would come out from behind his panelled door again and see how bad it was. Our boss kept saying, "Remember to work fast; the more windows you do, the more you make." After a while I noticed that the paint was cracking as it dried and falling off in little flakes. One of the guys pointed this out to him and he said, "Well, it only has to last until Christmas." He finished the window in a hurry. The paint was flaking off noticeably by the time he was done. He hustled us off to the car after a quick wave goodbye to the secretaries. He reminded me of one of those con men who writes bad checks with special ink that disappears as soon as he's out of reach.

Back at the office he loaded us up with equipment and a list of addresses and sent us off in groups of three. I had two guys in my group, Bob and Tony. Tony was real good looking, dark hair and a nice build and the prettiest smile I've ever seen. Bob had long ratty hair and scummy teeth. We stood in the parking lot outside the office building and made our plans. Tony had a van, which we figured would be most practical, and Bob had some dope, which was practical, too. We loaded our stuff in the van and Bob lit a joint and we were on our way.

We did three jobs that afternoon: An ice-cream parlor, a laundromat, and a chicken franchise, all of them complete with flaking Santas and watery snow. We made a lot of money and felt like thieves. I kept waiting for people to get mad at us for the lousy jobs, but they were real nice and Christmassy about the whole thing. That just made it worse. I felt especially bad about the ice-cream parlor because there were all these little kids who stood around and watched us like we were pros or something. They'd get up real close to the glass and I'd hold my breath, afraid that one of them would say something about the paint cracking. They didn't say a word.

By the time we were done, Bob and Tony and I weren't speaking. We were pissed off at each other, and even more pissed off at ourselves. We had to go back to the office and give the boss the checks for the jobs so he would work out his percentage.

We painted windows together for five days, arguing about technique and trying to figure out how to get the paint to stop flaking.

On Monday morning we gathered at the office to pick up our checks and begin a new week of work. There was a whole new set of people in the office; the boss and his secretary were gone. We asked the new secretary where they'd gone, and she just shrugged.

The sun makes brilliant points in my eyes, stippling my vision, annoying me like a small cloud of insects, so that I am

frowning when I look at Darrell. He releases my arm as suddenly as he had grabbed it. His expression is a welter of shadow and remorse, all anger departed. His mouth works silently, in apology? He rises and is gone before I can find my voice.

★

After that first time we made love, I tried to figure out what the arrangement was going to be. At first I thought maybe I felt lost because it was such an indifferent time of year. The weather wasn't hot and it wasn't cold, and Gary's and my relationship was in the same condition. It just sort of went on and on, and nobody ever said anything about it or paid much attention to it. I tagged along. When I was alone I would think of questions to ask Gary, but there was something about him that kept me from asking. It was sort of the same feeling you get when you're really loaded and lost, and there's nobody but a cop to ask directions from. You just don't do it. Eventually you find your way, but it takes a hell of a long time. So after that first time we fucked a lot, like it had been arranged that way for us. We had to schedule our activities around our mothers' schedules, which meant afternoon sex most of the time. Gary had a little sister to worry about, too, so we usually made it at my place. I got sick of sunlight. I wanted to make it in the dark because he made me feel so goddamn self-conscious. I hung around Gary and Dan's ceramics studio a lot. We might have fucked in the studio except that Dan was there every afternoon, and besides it was really cold in that old storefront. We did it in the bathroom once even though Dan was around, but it was more of a laugh than anything else. We did it with just our pants pulled down, and right in the middle of it I backed up against cold porcelain.

✶

So maybe he tried to keep it simple and nothing would stay simple. Maybe everything felt like a mistake, maybe he took the wrong bus, the wrong road. Maybe he tried to call me from somewhere and couldn't find the number. Darrell would do that, not be able to find the number. First he lost the genetic gamble; then he lost the ability to deal with the loss. I know he smashed the mirror before he left.

3.

We've always lived in apartments, Mom and Dan and I. Dan claims we had a house once, but I don't remember any of that. Mom won't talk about it. She was never any good at explaining things. Dan pieces things together as best he can and then tells me about it. He has lots of theories. He's three years older than me, and claims he can remember all kinds of details. He says he remembers Dad. I have to take it all on faith. But I can remember those apartment houses. The first one was called Coral Shores and was painted the sort of orange-pink color that you see on the fingernails of dopey middle-aged ladies in cheap department stores. Mom used to tell me how I'd yell and bounce up and down in the car when I caught sight of that atrocity of an apartment house; I'd point at it and grin, and she'd say, sure kid, there's home, you've got it right. We lived on the second floor, and I'd play out along the balcony. The balcony had a fancy metal railing that was painted the same orange-pink color as the stucco facade, and I used to sit there with my legs dangling over the edge and play suicide with my Betsy-Wetsy doll. Or I'd play high-diver; both games involved dropping Betsy from the balcony, it's just that with suicide she went straight down and hit the concrete, and with high-diver she went flying in an arc so she'd land in the pool. When I got bored with that, I'd sit on the balcony with my hands wrapped around the railing and watch the birds shit on the palm fronds that were just beyond my reach. There were palm trees bordering the courtyard all around. The color of the goddamn place was enough to underline the idiotic name, but somebody had to add one more tropical touch.

The second place we lived in was the good one. It was called Country Corral. I guess they called it that because there were some ragged orange groves in the area which gave it a rural atmosphere. By the time we moved again, the orange groves were gone and there was nothing but suburbs for miles around. But the years we spent there were just fine. Me and Dan were cowboys and Indians most of the time. When we got home from school we'd get our gear out and have ambushes in the orange groves. There were plenty of rowdy little kids in that neighborhood, and we'd have these great gang wars. The orange groves were great for a lot of things; birds had a habit of dropping feathers there, so we always had plenty to go around for all the Indians, plus nobody seemed to want the fruit that fell off the trees, which meant lots of ammo when the wars got hot. I got bashed in the head with moldy oranges many times, but I also did a lot of bashing myself. Another big plus was that in the summer when the streets were too hot to mess with and you had other things on your mind than softball, you could run around naked in the groves. We'd run around in there all dappled like leopards from the sun cutting through the trees, and nobody's parents ever ventured to come after us;

they probably never even guessed what we were up to. We played jungle doctor and wild natives, and once or twice we came upon what looked to us like adults making it in the soft dirt. We prided ourselves on being able to hide behind the rustling of the leaves, upon never cracking a twig. We were damn good. Once I even sneaked up on my brother, came within five feet of him without him ever noticing. He was beating off with another little kid. I was careful never to say anything about that to him or his friends. He would have kicked shit out of me if I had. But I was proud of myself for being able to creep around like that.

We moved away from Country Corral when I was eleven. We moved frequently after that because Mom had become a drunk by then and couldn't keep a job for very long. We saw a whole tour of apartment houses: Sunset Manor, Park Place, Ambassador Apartments, Palm Drive Apartments, Polynesian Village, Villa La Palma. Villa La Palma was the last one I lived in with my mom; after that, she continued the tour by herself.

Possibilities. He told me there were possibilities. If only. If you would. He sat with his hands wrenched together. Such violence in his hands. He was having difficulty speaking, having difficulty controlling the muscles in his face. He came back to the word possibilities like a sleepwalker.

My first apartment was in an old white frame house that had been divided into units of various sizes. Mine was the smallest of the lot; it was in the attic. I had a fine view. The house was on a hill in a quiet neighborhood. The area was populated by blacks and students mostly. I think we were on the border of some ghetto, but it seemed friendly enough. There were lots of old trees and a generous supply of children who seemed to shape their lives around that hill. I could see them biking and roller-skating and chasing baseballs down the hill until after dark. When the wind blew, the sound of the trees smoothed away the noise of the traffic below us.

I really loved that apartment. It was basically one room, with a kitchen area toward the street side and a sleeping area toward the back. There was a tiny bathroom, which I painted green, and a walk-in closet. The main room had slanting low ceilings that just barely cleared my head. I painted that room white. I got an old wooden table and painted it red. The floor was your typical spotted linoleum, not very interesting by itself, so I got a braided rug that Mom had kept rolled up for years. I also found a patchwork quilt that needed mending and fixed it, and I got some decent pillows at a rummage sale, and a great overstuffed couch. I bought a bunch of houseplants at K-Mart and put them in pots that Gary and Dan had made. I hung my own paintings and drawings on the walls. When it was finished, that apartment looked really fine, especially in the morning when the sun came in the windows and made bright patches on the floor.

I wasn't the only one who was arranging my own place. Dan had been living in an apartment with a roommate for a long time and he'd gotten sick of it, so a few weeks before I moved into my place, he moved into the ceramics studio. While I was painting my apartment, he was building a loft in the back of the storefront. Gary and I kicked sawdust around the concrete floor and talked to Dan as he hammered and sanded. We got to talking about living alone. All of us agreed that it was best to have a place to yourself and to have a few friends who had their own places, too, and that everybody should be busy doing something interesting.

I remember looking through dirty glass at grey sky, a span of empty telephone wires motionless across the treetops. I focused on the glass and saw how rain and dust had stained it. You had no pictures on your walls. Your windows were slowly becoming blind and you made no attempt to save them; your walls had a glacial tone. From the instant I stepped into the place I had a sense of damage. Could you have sat alone and looked out your window without noticing that the details of your view were fading?

I never even bothered to mention to Gary the possibility of living together. I learned fast how to gauge his silences. Some you could interrupt with words like "eat" and "fuck", but most were best left alone. I had to watch for visual cues. Like the way he didn't look at me when he talked about everyone having a place of their own. Since I was included in the conversation, I was included in the plans; but because eye contact was made only between Gary and Dan or me and Dan, I knew I'd better not approach Gary with a "we" during a lull in the conversation. I watched the side of his face and waited. He kept a cool focus on either Dan or the new loft.

He knew I'd take him in, even though I never said a word about it.

Gary watched Dan hammer nails into the loft. The nails slipped into the wood the way they might slip into flesh, clean and easy, and Gary watched with respect.

"Found a place?" said Dan between nails.

"Maybe," said Gary.

It was the first I'd heard, but I wasn't going to say anything.

"Where?"

"On Mountain View, near Lake."

"Lots of trees."

"Yeah."

"Nice."

"I'll get it if these other people can't come up with a deposit by tomorrow."

I wanted to ask him what the place was like, but I didn't think I could sound casual.

I was tracing the progress of the boat on the water with difficulty. The sun was bright on the water, bright and irregular and sharp as broken glass reflecting, and I kept losing the tiny white triangle of sail in the brightness. The boat seemed to be scudding along the rim of the pool, but I couldn't follow it. It seemed to be having trouble with the wind. Darrell was trying to tell me something, and I was watching the boat.

I helped Gary move into the place on Mountain View. My first impression was: Pit. Grimy stuff on the walls, goo on the floors, you name it. I didn't volunteer my services, and Gary seemed too absorbed in the novelty of his own place to mind. I helped him pile his stuff in a corner and split. I didn't see him for two days, and then I got a call.

"Come see it."

I did.

I was surprised. Gary's space at his mother's house had been like the storage room at a Greyhound depot, cramped and colorless. The apartment was elegant. I hadn't seen this side of Gary before. And this place was clean. More than clean, in fact. It was immaculate. Gary had painted the living room walls pale green and replaced the curtains with new blinds, and the sun slanted through the blinds very delicately and glowed on the wood floor. Somewhere Gary had found an oriental rug.

He watched me examine the rug.

He had painted the bedroom the color of bamboo and cleaned the woodwork so that it stood out dark against the walls, and put up white curtains. Somewhere he had found a white quilt.

He watched me examine the quilt.

I hadn't seen the bathroom on my first visit. I hadn't known a bathroom could be so beautiful. This one had deep blue tiles on the walls up to the level of the sink, and above the tile Gary had painted the walls white. The bathtub was one of the old ones with feet.

"I like the high ceilings, but they're a bitch to paint," Gary said.

I wandered through the rooms again. His pots were arranged carefully in every room. The place was airy and pleasant.

Gary fixed us tea in his freshly painted kitchen. We sat at the table in silence. I fiddled with my cup. He rubbed his cheek and gazed through the door. I felt like I'd just been through a very intense conversation.

"Want to fuck?" he asked.

I guess he was pretty tired from all that moving and cleaning and painting, because he fell asleep right after we made it in the bamboo room with the white quilt pulled aside. He fell asleep with his face up against my neck, and the warmth of his breath against my neck started a sort of tight feeling in the pit of my stomach, a funny tight feeling like I get from drinking too much coffee. I didn't want to move, though; I couldn't really with Gary pinning me like that. So I was still except for the buzz in my stomach, and I listened to Gary's breathing and afternoon sounds muted by the closed window. I heard a motorcycle go by. Gary started to feel heavy. I sneezed and felt Gary's cock slip out, and a wet spot began to spread on the sheet under me. The spot began to feel cold. *So he caught me by the arm and backed me up against the wall, not hurting me, just restraining me, and he demanded to know what was going on. He was trying very hard to make it sound like a reasonable request. But he was breathing in short, sucking gasps; breathing like no reasonable man. I was afraid to look past him. I heard people moving along, heard no sounds of hesitation, no hint of intervention from those people passing by.*

4.

We started taking classes in January. I signed up for basic drawing and photography. Dan and Gary took over the ceramics lab. Except for the studios and labs, the campus was a real dump. The old buildings were okay because you could tell they had a history to them, but the guys who designed the new ones must have been born dead. The new buildings looked like oversized computers or fancy packing crates. Maybe they reflected some-body's educational philosophy, but they didn't do much for me. Somebody had tried to cheer the place up by installing mirror pools along the front walkway of the college, but they'd painted the things that absurd shade of blue you find on postcards of the Los Angeles skyline. Bogus blue. I think the color aroused a universal con-tempt. Sparrows pooped in the water, dogs skirmished there, and students made boats from their test papers and watched them disintegrate.

But the studios and labs were nice. I liked to go from darkroom to ceramics lab to painting studio because the atmosphere was so different in each one. The darkroom was in the basement of Smith building. I liked the way you had to go through a twisting little corridor to get to the darkness without the light following you in. I liked the underground feeling and the smell of chemicals, and the fishtank look of people working in the dark, and the swish of paper in water. People didn't talk much in there, and I liked that, too.

The ceramics lab was completely different. That place was hardly ever quiet except late in the afternoon when everyone but the fanatics had gone home. When lots of people were there you could just walk in and latch on to a conversation, or better yet, a story. People were always hanging around in the glaze room or standing by the kilns on cold days and shooting the bull. Potters are a weird bunch. They can lead very conventional lives for years, and then somebody teaches them to throw and they get hooked. Give up everything and spend all their time in the ceramics lab making pots. And they tell stories about what they did before they got hooked. The guy who taught the course at City had been a senior in biology, headed for medical school when he took a ceramics course as a mick. Another guy drove a semi. Another guy told good stories about being the token black at some New England college. The ceramics lab was wide open, unlike the darkroom. It had an enormous room with about sixteen wheels and a couple of broad tables to work on, and walls of big clay-colored bricks, and high ceilings with windows running just below them so that you couldn't look outside and nobody could look in except through the doors. Light filtered down upon everyone as they worked, gentle as claydust. The claydust settled over everyone and everything in the lab, and when the pots had been thrown and glazed and put in the kilns for firing and there was nothing to hang around for, people trailed off for coffee and tracked clay to the cafeteria.

The painting studios were downright exclusive, mostly because of the nudes. A lot of the drawing and painting teachers were real keep-it-tight types, and they went into fits if a stranger happened in upon a session that involved a model. They didn't seem to mind so much about male models (nor did the models), but let an uninvited male lay eyes on a female nude and Violation had occurred. More than once I saw a teacher shoot outraged looks at an interloper or shout, jarring the model from her daydream and ruining many a contour drawing. People drew and painted in those studios; they didn't talk. Talk would have been like a fly in an operating room. A studio was quiet except for whispered advice from teacher to student, and people rarely broke the hush with a cough or the moving of a chair. They were producing Art. The model held her pose in a haze of light and boredom while the teacher prowled, supervising. I always chose a corner near the door to work in. Even though I sort of liked the intensity, I needed to feel that I could escape unobserved.

The routes I took to avoid him: the pedestrian bridge between Smith and Moline buildings, the corridor through the music building, the interconnecting classrooms on the first floor of Farnsworth Hall that I went sneaking through on my way to drawing class so that Darrell wouldn't see me from his lookout by the ceramics lab. It was a war that we never spoke of, an issue of visibility and invisibility, a nightmare of exposure. I couldn't stand his eyes upon me, yet he stationed himself so that I couldn't avoid them. He watched me insatiably. His lookout points: the benches by the mirror pools, the steps next to the ceramics lab, the corner table in the cafeteria, any area that I

habitually passed through on my way to and from classes. He
usually saw me before I saw him because he was primed for
watching; he seemed nearly clairvoyant in his ability to antici-
pate my movements. I would be talking to someone, thinking I
was free, when in the instant of a gesture I would find myself
pinioned by his gaze. In the distance I would see him watching,
his face turned full upon me, the sense of his eyes as distinct
upon my skin as the touch of an enemy's hand.

I didn't know what to make of Gary sometimes. I got the
feeling every now and then that he wanted to hurt me,
really hurt me. He got perverse sometimes. Like the time
we were at his mother's house watching a stupid game show
on TV and eating grilled cheese sandwiches and not saying
anything, not saying anything at all. Usually when we were
alone he would turn on either the stereo or the TV, and he
never said much of anything except when he had to, like
"Do you want a grilled cheese sandwich?" That was all he'd
said to me since we'd set foot in the house. We sat on the
awful red plush carpet in the living room and got greasy up
to our wrists eating sandwiches in silence except for the
game show nagging at our ears. When he was done with his
sandwich, he wiped his hands on the carpet, real long and
slow, and then he slid his hand up my thigh and grabbed my
twat and I felt embarrassed because my mouth was full and
my hands were all shiny with grease. He still didn't say
anything, he just went for the back of my dress and unzipped it and pulled it down around my hips and shoved me
down on my back before I could wipe my hands. The best I
could do was swallow what was in my mouth while he was
yanking his pants down. As soon as he had his pants off he
was working his way into me and I had my fingers deep in
the carpet, and he felt good in me, but my mind kept
shooting down to the base of my spine and locking there in

a spot of pain. When he was coming I was still locked down there in that spot of pain and hanging on to that ugly carpet. He got off me and I realized what it was; it was my zipper digging at the base of my spine, and there was a nasty bloody place where the metal had gouged me. I told Gary to look, and he looked and got up and went for a bandaid. He came back with it and gave it to me, and then he picked up the plate where the sandwiches had been and he disappeared into the kitchen, and he didn't say anything at all.

✳

Losers and crazies all over campus. Thousands of them. I had dreams at night about looking for Gary and having to go through forests of losers and crazies. On my way from darkroom to ceramics lab I'd glance into classrooms as I walked by, and they'd be packed in there, gazing out available doors and windows, mouths hanging loose as in sleep. In the quad I'd pass clusters of losers doing their thing: monitoring passing strangers, watching fearfully for crazies. The crazies were real noticeable. They excited everybody's radar. You could feel them veering toward you, or hear them, depending upon their style. There was one guy, Jimmy the ex-con, who broadcast all his thoughts in his deep-South drawl or sang real loud, and scared everybody with his crazy stare. He'd stare at anybody. He had pimples on his pimples, and he was dirty. Girls were afraid he'd come up and talk to them, and maybe grab a tit. I don't know what the guys thought. I'd seen them standing around in their khaki pants looking nervous, doing a little khaki shuffle and trying not to look beyond the nucleus of their group.

I guess the khaki contingent thought I was on the weird side, too. I suppose I was. Since I'd moved into my own place, my style had evolved from shorty-short embroidered dresses and flaming tights to slinky dresses and high-heeled shoes. In my heels I stood about six-three, a good eight inches taller than Gary. The khakis rubbernecked like mad when I walked by. I was taller than any of them.

I saw him downtown once. He was walking along, watching the shopkeepers change the season in store windows, his shabby image following him in the plate glass. I hid myself in the crowd by a bus bench hoping he wouldn't see me, and he didn't; he walked by us as if we were a grove of trees. When the bus came, I got on it and rode for several miles along the boulevard, not knowing why I wanted so brutally to get away.

I was really liking that darkroom. You couldn't tell what time it was down there unless you asked somebody, and hardly anybody spoke. So it was like time didn't exist, like you had walked into a dream. Everything was indistinct in a nice way. I'd sort of fade out while I worked with the enlarger, daydreaming over paper and strips of film, aware of people moving silently around me but not seeing them. I'd fool with the enlarger until I was half blind, and then I went through the ritual of recovering my sight. This was the part I liked the best. I'd take my empty paper to the trough where the chemicals were lined up in trays, and I'd slip my paper into the first tray. Then I'd rock the tray and coax it, listening to the water gurgle somewhere in the trough, and I'd hum a little tune to myself and watch my paper, and out of the chemical depths visions would emerge, undeniable visions in black and white. My visions went from tray to tray, through the dryer and into the drawer where I finally claimed them. I put them in a manila envelope and carried them around with me so I could take them out and look at them when I felt like it.

I had pictures of Gary, and pictures of me that I took with a tripod and timer because I couldn't stand to have someone squinting at me from behind a camera. I had pictures of Dan bracing himself against clay, the potter's wheel a blur. Gary with his sleeves rolled up. Me with my hair in my face. Dan lighting a cigarette, frowning. Me reclining on my overstuffed couch, looking at the camera. Me sitting on the couch naked, looking as though I didn't have time to arrange myself before the shutter closed. Gary touching the rim of a pot with his index finger, looking satisfied. The veins standing out along Dan's arms as he hefts a very large pot, grinning.

I tried to imagine him running, but Darrell was no runner. Gravity reproached him at every step. So how did he escape? How long did it take me to go from desk to door? I expected to see him in retreat, but like a dreamer I was deceived. No report of his feet on the stairs. From the landing I looked to the street. The street was naked as the barrel of a gun, and all around me there was silence.

I was downtown one evening walking off this nastiness that had started in my stomach when I tried to reach Gary. I didn't feel right about just dropping by his apartment, so I'd called to see what was up. Well, the line was busy for a while, and when I tried again it rang for a long time. It rang until I gave up. My stomach told me something was wrong and I ignored it. I figured he was on his way over or something. I figured wrong.

So I went downtown. My stomach was jumping all over the place, but walking helped some. I tried looking in store windows at clothes and things to take my mind off Gary, but that didn't help at all. After a while I had the feeling I was being followed by this guy. I noticed him out of the corner of my eye as I was looking at the fabrics in the window of Maxine's. He was sort of looking at the display in the used book store, but something in the way he was standing said he was watching me. He looked kind of familiar. I walked a little further and stopped at a fresh window, and he did the same, staying about two windows behind me, and I recognized him as one of the losers in photography class. I needed some diversion, so I waved to him. At first he pretended like he didn't notice, but after a minute he caught up with me.

He had a real sad face, so I told him stories to cheer him up. I told him about the time I was in Juvie, and the time I was a chauffeur for a vegetable. He strolled along with me and listened without saying anything, and he began to laugh at things I said. I started to feel better. He interrupted to tell me about the time he was drunk and wandered into a massage parlor just to see what would happen. It was a long, involved story, and I could tell by the way he went into detail that he'd thought about this story a lot. I started to get bored and just looked at him instead of listening, and I noticed how pale and moist his face was. His hair was real dark and limp, and his nose looked waxy and a little bit lumpy. He was wearing a grey sweatshirt with a hood, and a dark blue windbreaker over that. He slouched real bad. That's how I'd recognized him, by his slouch. He was the baggy guy who spent a lot of time busying himself in the darkroom, talking to no one, invisible except for his slouch. Harmless.

So when I started back home again and he followed, I didn't feel nervous about it. A couple of times he asked if it was alright for him to walk with me. Did I mind? He seemed real pleased to be exchanging stories and walking together like friends.

My stomach had settled down. In fact, it had settled into a smooth angry feeling. What with my new friend to reassure me, I was actually getting pissed off at Gary. I thought about Gary and half-listened to my darkroom friend as he related some incident of campus politics.

"It shouldn't be like that, right?" he said.

"Right," I said, as if I knew what he was talking about.

When we arrived at my street he hesitated. I asked him for the time. 9:30, and I didn't want to be alone. I invited him in for tea. He seemed grateful.

I can't remember what we talked about. We told a lot of stories, I guess. We sat opposite each other at my little red table, and much of the time as he talked I stared over his shoulder at the telephone. I don't know if he noticed. He never made a move to touch me; our knees didn't even touch under the table. The quality of the darkness outside didn't change at all. We drank an awful lot of tea.

It was after four when he left.

The next day I slept through the morning and into the afternoon so that I missed photography class. It felt good. I opened the window to check the weather. It was bright and sunny and just a little bit cool, and Gary was coming up the walk. My stomach went cold and I got this seeping sensation in my armpits.

I was trying to think when I let him in, but I lost it soon after that. I wanted to rearrange my theories about our relationship and maybe work up the nerve to ask a few questions. But the minute he was in my apartment I felt naked. He stood and looked at me and I held my robe around myself, wondering what to do and if I could do it gracefully. I couldn't help looking at his body, compact as a fist. He changed his stance so I could see his hard-on. Subtle. I began to feel a change in my knees, and there was this crumpling feeling deep inside. The second I looked away, he came after me.

His hands were powdery soft and warm.

"Been working in the ceramics lab?"

"Mm."

"Gary . . ."

"Lie down."

The sun is shifting over me, I want to get out of the shade out of the wind, but Darrell is talking to me and to be polite I must stay. I want to lie down in the sun. I can almost feel the sun on my skin, warm. Eyes closed. But I must keep my eyes open for Darrell. I put one hand out of the shade and feel my skin taking the warmth. For a moment my lips relax with desire. I realize, too late, that my mouth is open and my eyes are beginning to stare.

"God!"

Gary rolled off of me and fell asleep. I was just lying there trying to figure out how I felt. My stomach was funny again, and I wanted to get up and get dressed, but I didn't want to wake Gary. So I stayed put. I don't know how long I was lying there when I heard footsteps on the stairs outside and somebody knocked softly on my door. I pulled the covers over me and waited, listening. Whoever was out there waited, too. I heard the floor creak where the person was standing, and then silence again. I wondered if they would try to open the door. For a moment I was scared because the door wasn't locked and whoever it was could just waltz right in. A murderer? A Jehovah's Witness? I prayed that Gary wouldn't roll over or sneeze. The knocking started again, softly, and then stopped, and I swear I heard someone breathing out there. Then the floor creaked again and whoever it was went down the stairs and went away. I moved just enough to get a glimpse of the clock. Two in the afternoon. I wanted to go to the darkroom.

Gary woke up as I was getting out of bed and caught my wrist.

"What's up?" he said, holding me so that I couldn't stand up straight and my breasts dangled where he could stare at them, which he did. I couldn't reach my robe, so I reached with my free hand for the sheets, but Gary snatched that hand and pulled me down even more.

"I'm not comfortable standing this way."

"I wish I were standing behind you right now so I could fuck you doggie-style."

"Gary."

"What." He yanked my arms just a little so that my breasts jiggled, and he never took his eyes off them.

"Stop staring at my tits."

"What's the matter?" He pulled me down next to him and rolled me over so that my back was to him, and he held my breasts too tightly as he rubbed his penis against my buttocks.

"You're hurting me and besides I want to go to school and get some work done."

He jabbed his penis into me. "You're dry."

"Then why not give me a chance to get into it before you start poking me?"

"Get into it then." He thrust even harder and held me down when I tried to move.

"Goddamn it, Gary!"

"Take it easy."

When he was done with that, he told me he would let me go to school if I would suck him off. Suck him off and get it over with in five or ten minutes or fuck him all afternoon, that was the deal. He was really being obnoxious and I didn't feel like sucking him or anybody off right then, but I wanted out. And I had to do it just the way he wanted, he said, or it wouldn't be worth sacrificing a whole afternoon of fucking for one blow job. I wanted to get dressed and ready to leave before doing it, but he insisted that I be naked.

He took me by the hair and told me to open my mouth, and he shoved it in as deep as he could. I was tempted to bite him, but I figured it might be bad for my health, so I just did the best job I could with him holding my hair twisted around his fingers. I did my best not to choke so he wouldn't get any satisfaction that way. When he came he told me to swallow it.

When he walked out, he left the door standing wide open, and he didn't even say goodbye.

Darrell. I went to the school authorities and got your address. They told me you were still registered. They didn't seem anxious at all. I kept your address in my pocket for days; my fingers found it over and over again. I took it out and looked at it, smudged and shiny pencil on an eroded scrap of paper. I'd seen you last on Thursday; the following Tuesday I took the bus downtown. I walked several blocks looking for your apartment; it was in one of those decaying Victorians. Your landlady was openly suspicious. She unlocked your door and showed me your rooms. I couldn't tell if the place was a mess because of a hasty departure or if it was a mess because

you are such a slob. The landlady said the tenants' business was none of her business and locked the door.

✶

I was in the darkroom by three. My thoughts were moving so fast my head felt like it was on fire. I wondered what my face looked like whenever I stepped into the light; were my lips pale? Did my jaw seem tense? Did I look angry or absorbed? I printed three portraits of myself and stared at them as they floated face-up in the fixer. I studied them for character. What would a stranger see? As my prints were drying, I went to the cafeteria for a drink. I could still taste chlorine. In the cafeteria I sipped coke and chewed the end of a straw and watched strangers. I watched the men closely and tried to guess which ones might be rapists. Would they work alone or in gangs? Most of them looked like the gang type.

Someone was looking through glass at me, hands shaped like a diver's mask around his eyes, hands pressed dark against the window. I couldn't see his eyes, but I knew he was looking at me. I had my feet resting on a chair, and my skirt draped casually, maybe too casually, over my legs, so I sat up straight and rearranged my clothes. I sipped my coke and pretended that the walls were concrete, not glass. He drew back from the window and I recognized him, but pretended not to see. The windbreaker, the slouch. Holding a camera like an excuse. He moved away, into the brilliance of the patio and sat down at one of the picnic tables, facing me. Trouble. Maybe not. Maybe he was watching someone else. Staking out a subject. The photography instructor encouraged us to do that. He wasn't watching me, then. I was just being self-conscious, as usual. Dumb thing to do. I finished my coke and went out the side door.

I went back to the darkroom for my prints. One of them wasn't as clear as I would have liked, so I made a new print, and while I was working on it the slouchy guy showed up. This made me nervous. I said hello very casually and then acted like I was concentrating hard and didn't want to be disturbed. That routine works with 50% of them, but he turned out to be one of the difficult 50%. He kept hanging around, not even making an attempt to look like he was doing something. This was a very bad sign. I had to say something.

"That was some talk we had last night, wasn't it?"

"It was wonderful." He looked down at his feet.

"Going to do some work?" I really wanted him to work and stop giving me so much attention. It was getting late and most everybody had gone home for dinner or whatever, so it was just me and this guy and the TA, who was off in some other part of the lab, so we were pretty much alone.

"Do you mind if I work with you?"

"Of course not! This is public property, right?" I put on my cheery voice to make everything seem light and fine. No intensity here. It didn't work.

"You're sure?"

"Of course! Look, Daniel ..."

"Darrell."

"Well, look, Darrell, it was real nice talking to you last night. You tell some fine stories, but our talk didn't change anything, right? I mean it doesn't make the darkroom private, and you don't have to ask my permission to use it. You know what I mean?"

He just stood there, kind of half turned away like he couldn't decide whether to stay or go, and stared at me, completely still except for a strand of hair creeping down his forehead. He looked kind of crazy. I felt I'd better distract him.

"You got something you're thinking of printing? I'd sort of like to see what you do." I couldn't remember seeing any of his work in class.

He was still staring. He hadn't moved. The dim light over the enlarger made his skin look yellow and dead. I couldn't help being distracted by the way the light lay flat upon his face, but I tried to concentrate on his eyes; I tried to make it seem like a normal conversation between two students. When he finally moved he seemed very deliberate and sad.

"I'll show you one of my contact sheets if you'd really like to see it," he said, looking at me out of the corner of his eye.

"I would." I said, and I followed him out of the darkroom to the row of lockers just outside. He opened his locker and took out a sheaf of contact sheets.

"Let's sit down at the table." I suggested. He followed me over to the table and sat down. Then he thumbed through his contact sheets, frowning a little. After much deliberation he found one he apparently liked, examined it for a moment, and shyly handed it to me.

They were not striking photographs. Most of them were badly framed shots of old houses, odd trees, and various shop windows. There were a few blurry attempts at a panorama of the city, taken at night from one of those roadside vantage points in the mountains. In none of them were any people visible.

Darrell watched me as I looked at his pictures, so I tried to seem really interested. I asked a lot of questions. What kind of film was he using? At what speed? What effect was he trying to achieve? I felt stupid and helpless asking him those questions, but I didn't know what to say. He was still watching me from the corners of his eyes. I can't remember how he answered. Finally he stood up and took the contact sheets from my hand and declared, "You don't really like them, do you?" I assured him that I did, avoiding his eyes as I said so, pointing to the images as I explained how there was a nice eerie quality to the pictures of the houses especially, a really stark quality. I almost had myself convinced. I helped him select a photo to print, and he went off, almost enthusiastically, to print it.

I made like I was going to continue working. While Darrell busied himself with an enlarger, I took my prints out of the last tray and put them in a pan, arranged them and held them up to the light for a look. When I saw that Darrell had forgotten me for a moment, I slipped out of the darkroom. I tried not to hurry because I figured he'd notice. I put my prints in the dryer and checked around to make sure I had everything put away, listened for a moment for any sounds of hesitation, took my jacket off the hook and split. I don't think I started breathing again until I was up the stairs and out the door.

The sun had gone down while I was in the darkroom and the air was cold, so I pulled on my jacket and hustled along the sidewalk. I was kind of hungry and I didn't want to go home, so I headed for the Big Boy across the street. I needed to think. I went into the restaurant and took a little table at the end of some booths. I was lucky to get the table at all. I nabbed it as a couple got up to leave. It was so busy in there that the waitress didn't even try to say hello as she cleared the table, and there was a line of sweat glistening along her upper lip. She left me sitting in a little cloud of hairspray scent. I looked at the menu even though I already knew I was going to have a hamburger and a glass of milk, and then I put the menu back in its little holder and checked out the people sitting around me. The lighting in the place was just like the lighting in city buses at night, in fact I sort of felt like I was sitting on a bus. The seats were like bus seats, too, those vinyl padded numbers that make you bounce involuntarily when you sit down. The people nearest me were seated with their backs to me, so I could only see the backs of their heads or the sides of their faces when they turned to talk to each other. And the place was full of students; I could tell by the stacks of books and notebooks on the tables and counters. I figured it was busy because people were just getting out of late afternoon classes and wanted dinner, or else they were killing time before night classes. Everybody was talking, talking, talking, or else hiding behind a book. I didn't have a book to hide behind. If I hadn't been so hungry, I might have left. I was thinking about leaving when the waitress showed up with pad and pen. I committed myself to a hamburger and sat there feeling dumb.

This couple in front of me started playing post office or something right there in the booth. I tried not to watch, but the girl kept punctuating each kiss with a shrill little scream. I guess nobody else could really hear them because the restaurant was so noisy, and I was just lucky to be sitting so close. I started concentrating on the activity outside. While I was sitting there, the street started filling up with cars. I started to count the number of times they circled, looking for parking spaces. The sidewalk was getting crowded, too, and I noticed people leaving their coffee cups on the counter and gathering up their books. By the time the waitress delivered my hamburger, the restaurant was more than half empty.

I was glad to have that hamburger to keep me busy. I took a big bite out of it. Some juice got away from me and dripped down my chin, so I fumbled the burger to my plate and grabbed a napkin and cleaned up the drip just as it was threatening my blouse. I picked up the hamburger again and was about to take another bite when my eyes focused on an anxious face passing through the crowd on the sidewalk. Darrell.

I put the hamburger down and took a sip of milk, glancing over the rim of my glass at Darrell as he passed along the window. He was looking around. I prayed he wouldn't look in the window and see me. I needed to think, and I couldn't think if he came in and started staring at me again. I watched him reach the end of the long window and disappear.

I finished that burger as fast as I could, chugged the milk, and scooted off the padded seat. While the girl rang up the bill, I scanned the street. Not much going on. Just a few latecomers hurrying to class and some stray dudes strutting and hanging out by the hamburger stands across the boulevard. Time to go home.

A wind was coming up, and the night sky had that clear, velvety quality that comes with clean air. Little gusts caught me as I walked, lifting my hair and making my skirt billow out in front of me. It was really very pleasant. I could see people on the fourth floor balcony of Moline, leaning on the railing, looking out over the night. Though I couldn't identify them individually, I knew who they were. They were painting and drawing students taking a break from class. It gave me a good feeling to see them up there. I guess they were sort of my people because we were interested in the same things. I almost forgot where my car was because I was thinking about them, but I caught myself in time and headed for B Lot.

I always have trouble in parking lots. My car blurs into the mass of cars and I have to strain to see it. When I focused on it at last, my eyes zeroed in on a slip of yellow paper fluttering under a windshield wiper. A ticket or a flier. As I approached I saw that it was too individual a piece of paper to be either of those things; it was a note. Gary? I took it out from under the wiper and read:

> I hope I didn't upset you in the lab this afternoon. I never meant you any trouble or wanted to interrupt your work. Please forgive me. Just say the word and I won't trouble you any more.
>
> D.

The printing was large and childish, as if it were done with much effort. I read the note over again, folded it up and stuck it in my jacket pocket.

I ran up the wooden stairs to my apartment. In the darkness of the little entryway I almost tripped over a pot that had been left by my door, a note curled into its mouth. The note said:

> Why didn't you drop by the ceramics lab today? I tried to find you in the dark-room this afternoon, no go. When you didn't show up, I thought you might be sick, so I gave you a call, no answer. I thought I'd come by and check it out. What's up?
>
> What do you think of the glaze on this pot?
>
> It's an experiment. Keep it.
>
> Dan

I unlocked the door, picked up the pot, flicked on the light and went inside. I locked the door behind me automatically. First thing I had to do was find a place to put the new pot, which wasn't easy because I already had pots and plants and odds and ends in every available bit of space. I stood in the center of the room and stared for a few minutes, and then I gave up and stuck the pot on the kitchen table. I stripped off my jacket and threw it over the couch. I noticed the blinds were open and closed them. Then I decided the overhead light was too much, so I turned on the lamp on the coffee table and killed the overhead.

My stash was in my bag, and while I was getting it I took out my current manila envelope full of pictures. I rolled a joint over the envelope, lit up, sat back, and pulled out a handful of photos.

There was one picture in particular I wanted to study, one of Gary and me sitting on my couch. I sorted through the the photos until I found it. Then I took a good long hit and settled down to examine the situation. We are sitting on the couch. I look unprepared, as usual. My knees point off to the right, my feet are flat on the floor, but my torso twists to the left. My arms extend to either side of me along the top of the couch. My shoulders look tense. My face is turned to the left, but my eyes are on the camera, two black points. Gary is to my left. He is sitting, legs crossed, hands behind his head, casual. He is looking away from the camera, away from me. His expression is abstracted. Both of us are handsome. Both of us are expensively dressed. The clothes drape well, but they drape better on him. He looks European, even cosmopolitan. I am hopelessly American. The busiest part of the picture is the background. My plants are doing a crowd scene. Just above our heads is a shelf crammed with pots and knickknacks, very busy.

I was dissatisfied with that picture and went on to the next. This was a portrait of Gary, taken from the same angle. He is completely deadpan. He is sitting up, legs crossed, hands folded over his crotch, staring straight at the camera. His shirt is unbuttoned almost to the waist and his chest hair is shadowy against the fabric. After taking this one, I wouldn't let him pose anymore. He was too unnerving.

The joint had gone out, so I relit it, got too much smoke, and went into a coughing fit. I dumped my pictures on the coffee table. When I stopped coughing, I realized that I was really kind of tired, so I got ready for bed as fast as I could and promptly went to sleep.

I awoke to the sound of rain spattering my windows and nearly went under again; I needed to know what time it was in order to stop the disorientation brought on by rain. I focused on my clock. Nine-thirty. I forced myself out of the warmth, wrapped myself in my terrycloth robe, went to the front windows, opened the blinds. The street was a grey blur. The trees were rearing and plunging in the wind, dark masses. I saw that one of the larger branches had fallen, and I worried about my car. I opened the window enough to lean out so I could see it. It looked okay. I was soaked. I dripped all the way to the bathroom and took a hot shower, then I wrapped my hair in a towel and put on a fresh robe and sat over a cup of coffee, feeling steamy warm and comfortable. The rain came down steadily as I dressed.

B Lot was full of streaming cars and giant puddles. A few people sprinted toward shelter, leaping puddles, clinging to books. I opened my umbrella and picked my way through the lot, careful not to spoil my boots. The balconies of Moline building were empty, and the doors were shut. In spite of my umbrella I was getting wet. I went straight to the ceramics lab.

Phil was lecturing a class, demonstrating something on one of the wheels toward the back of the lab, so I sneaked into the kiln room and stood alone by one of the two big kilns. It was intensely hot. I could smell the wool of my skirt drying. Lulled by the heat, I combed my hair and day-dreamed about nothing in particular. Pretty soon I heard the class dispersing, and then Dan was standing next to me.

"Hiya." he said, and gave me a little hug. "Where have you been?"

I pushed hair out of my face and winked at him.

"Got some plates and things in this one," he said, nodding at the kiln. He glanced at his watch. "Due out in about an hour and a half."

I continued to comb my hair. Dan lit a cigarette and leaned against the doorframe.

"Seen Mom lately?" I asked.

"Nope."

"Where's Gary?"

"I saw him in the cafeteria earlier. Should be here soon." Dan blew a smoke ring and watched it disintegrate.

"What are you doing for money?" he asked.

"I'm running out. What are you doing?"

"Little of this, little of that."

He was giving me his cowboy look. He squinted up his eyes and let his hair fall over his forehead just so, and he held his jaw kind of tight.

"Well, I'm going to go see Mom and ask for some help with the finances. Any messages?"

"Nope."

"Hey Dan."

"Mm?"

"Has Gary been messing around with somebody else? I

mean, have you seen him with any other girls? I just want to know. He's been a little strange lately."

I watched his face to see if he had anything to tell. He was maddeningly slow about answering me.

"Gary's my friend. You're my little sister. I don't want to be mixed up in your affairs."

I couldn't read his face. I gave up.

"Well, if you see him, tell him I'm around. I'll be in the darkroom."

"Okay. Why don't you check back after class and have a look at my new stuff?"

I put my comb away and tossed my hair back over my shoulders. Dan saw me to the door. I wanted him to leave so I could make up my mind privately whether I wanted to go to the cafeteria or to the darkroom. I didn't want to seem hung up about Gary. That never helped anything. Dan stood and smoked and watched the rain and I felt really awful. I cut through Moline building to avoid getting wet, and walked quickly across the quad to Smith. I was standing by the door, shaking out my umbrella, when a figure dressed head to knee in a yellow slicker confronted me.

"How are you?" he said.

I looked up at a damp, worried face.

"Did you get my note?" he asked before I could say anything.

"Uh, yes. I had to leave because I felt sick all of a sudden. It was no reflection on you."

I watched the frown disappear. He pulled the hood of his slicker off and stuck it under his arm. Then he took a kerchief out of his pocket and wiped his face thoroughly.

"Are you headed for class?" he asked after passing the kerchief over his mouth.

"Yeah." They never see the signs.

"May I walk with you?"

"Sure."

Darrell worked his way through the crowd with me. I stared hard at feet and green tile. I didn't want to see him, I didn't want to see anything. He was trying to make conversation, something about pictures, but I kept getting separated from him by jostling students and having to say "What?" after every statement he made. He gave up and we worked our way along in silence. On the stairs he tried again.

"I'd like to have a long talk with you another time. I enjoyed talking to you more than you can imagine."

I was glad that we were on the steps so that I had an excuse to look down at my feet, and not into his eyes which were seeking mine. We had to keep moving in order to get to class on time. We had to be careful where we stepped so that we wouldn't slip on the water tracked into the building. So my attention was divided into occasional glances, and with each glance I saw something I didn't want to see. He looked as though he barely had control of himself. The basement was a roar of voices and heels coming down on tile. He opened the door for me, and I felt awkward and confused. On ordinary days I opened my own doors. I wanted ordinary days. Some people in the class turned to look. The slouchy one and the tall girl, a connection. Me and Darrell. He sat next to me through the lecture, my face crawling with his eyes, my attention failing because it was divided, the lecture lost. I took the few notes I had and stuffed them into my bag. To Darrell's look I made some excuse about an appointment, and I left without doing any work.

I went back to the ceramics lab. The lab was at its busiest; some women were at the long table making coil pots, all of the wheels were occupied, and there were people standing around discussing design with Phil, making sketches on scraps of paper, pointing out details. Outside the light was pearly grey. The lab was warm and bright, and the students seemed oblivious to the rain, reminded of it only when a rain-drenched person entered. I leaned up against the wall just inside the door and scanned the room. Gary wasn't at any of the wheels, and neither was Dan. I walked along the rows of wheels, glancing at the lopsided pots spinning in the hands of the novices, stopping at the back door of the kiln room to see if Gary and Dan were there. A girl was warming her hands by the kiln, talking to a guy who was sketching a fish on the surface of an unfinished pot. They ignored me as I walked through. Gary and Dan weren't in the glaze room, either, but I could hear them shouting over the noise of the pug mill. I stood outside the door and listened to their conversation. They were talking about glazes, interjecting remarks about the consistency of the clay they were mixing. They had just started to work with porcelain, and they were comparing it to stoneware. They were completely absorbed in possibilities. I thought about interrupting them, but I realized I had nothing to say. So I turned around and walked back through the big room where the wheels were grinding away, and I went back into the rain.

5.

It was still raining on Saturday, the day I'd set aside to visit my mother. I had hoped for some sun, figuring that Villa La Palma would be less depressing on a clear day.

I had been staying away from my mother, communicating by phone mostly, and then not much, so I wasn't sure what she was up to, if anything. She had told me that she found a new job just after I moved out, and that it paid better than the last one. I hated Villa La Palma, but she liked the place, and she sounded at least stable when I talked to her on the phone. I dressed up nicely so I could impress her with my new image, and then I climbed into the Oldsmobile and drove off to see her.

The palm trees were dripping and rivulets of dirt had made their way out of the landscaping bed, across the sidewalk, and into the gutter. I stepped on snails that I couldn't avoid as I entered Villa La Palma. In the courtyard I could hear TVs jabbering through the rain. The lounge chairs by the swimming pool were wet and uninviting, and through the pocked surface of the water I could see leaves staining the bottom of the pool. I felt like turning around and leaving, but I made myself go upstairs and knock on my mother's door.

Mom answered the door in a wig, a caftan, and platform shoes.

"Ta daa!" she said. "Knocked you speechless, didn't I?"

I stepped inside and made a big production of walking around her and staring. 'Prosperous times?" I asked. She sure looked different. I mean, she still had bags under her eyes, but you could tell she'd been working on this new image. "New boyfriend?"

"Maybe. Want some coffee?"

"Sure."

She was treating me like a goddamned friend.

She hustled around in her kitchenette, getting mugs and cream. I sat down at the table and watched her to see if she was really happy about something or if this was just a front. I couldn't tell. She fluttered around like a cockatoo in a cage, telling me about how she was going to redecorate the apartment and all. When she finally sat down across from me, she wouldn't look me in the eyes. She'd look here and there, over my shoulder and out the window; she'd gaze into her coffee cup as she talked about what color she was going to paint the walls, and her eyes would flicker over mine when she asked a direct question. But never did her eyes come to rest on mine. I wanted to ask her if she'd stopped drinking so much, but I couldn't do it. I wanted to ask again, seriously, if she had a lover, but I couldn't do that, either. So I let her entertain me with talk about clothes and the apartment, and let her question me about school. I told her about Dan and Gary making pottery and I told her how I had been painting and drawing. I told her all about photography, too, and she only interrupted to ask questions. She asked to see my work sometime, and I told her that I'd bring her a portfolio.

She poured both of us a third cup of coffee while I fished around for a way to ask her for money. We sat in silence for a while. I stirred little whorls of cream through my coffee. She cleared her throat a couple of times. I decided not to ask her for money because she seemed so sad in spite of all the new stuff.

I took a sip of my coffee, but it was too hot. I felt like moving around a little, so I got up to look at some knick-knacks on a shelf. I heard Mom take a cigarette out of a pack and light up.

"The longer skirts look nice on you." she said to my back.

"Thanks." I said, picking up a little ceramic milkmaid and watching her shiny ceramic buckets fight the silver chains of her yoke.

"You really like school, don't you?"

"I never thought I would, but I do." I gave the milkmaid a shake, and her buckets clicked against her polished blue dress. She had a corny startled expression.

"Are you going to finish school? Get a degree?"

I put the milkmaid back on the shelf and picked up her mate, a little shepherd. "I thought I might go to an art school if I could get a scholarship."

I could hear Mom tapping her cigarette against the ashtray.

"I can help you out if you want." she said.

I put the shepherd back, went to Mom, and almost knocked her crazy wig off hugging her. She got tangled up in the sleeves of her caftan trying to rescue her wig and hug me at the same time.

✳

61

The rain continued through Sunday, but Monday was clear. I knew that it was a bright and sunny day the instant I woke up. On days like that I wake up early and I wake up feeling lucid. So on Monday I awoke at eight, full of energy and ready to do things. I bathed and dressed, fixed eggs and toast and tea for breakfast, and watched the little kids of the neighborhood walk down the hill to school while I ate. The sun came hot through the window and dried my hair as I sat at the table. After breakfast I made my bed and straightened up the apartment, watered my plants, and dusted everything.

I felt so good that I decided to reward myself by going shopping. Mom had given me a generous check, more than enough for my school needs. So around ten I put on my jacket and headed out the door.

I cruised downtown in the Oldsmobile, enjoying the combination of bright sun and cool air. Downtown the shops were just opening up and the parking lots were filling with cars. I turned off the main drag onto Lake. The Lake Avenue shops were the best in town, and in one of them was a pair of red boots that I wanted.

The salesgirl was less than friendly, as usual. She was standing over by a rack of skirts, arms folded, unsmiling, as I walked in. As a concession to politeness, I guess, she turned partially away before giving me the once-over instead of giving me a head-on stare. Satisfied once again that she looked better than the dope who had just walked in the door, she turned away from me and began to straighten the skirts on the rack.

When I am alone and being watched, I am conscious of being tall. I felt conspicuously tall as I browsed along the racks. The salesgirl had moved over to the cosmetics counter, keeping an eye on me. I pulled a satin blouse from the rack and held it up in front of the mirror. It looked awful. But I looked fine. I put the blouse back where I'd found it and went directly to the corner where the boots were, making a point to look down at the salesgirl as I passed her. She made a weak attempt at a smile.

My boots were still there, soft red leather boots that laced to the knee. Sixty bucks. The salesgirl started hovering behind me, so without looking at her I said that I wanted them in a size nine. She swished off to get the boots. I waited for her and thought about guilt feelings. My mother's money. The girl came back with the boots and watched as I put them on. She said something half-assed about how nice they were and I gave her a dirty look. She found something else to do. When I finished lacing the boots I went to the mirror. They were perfect, exactly what I wanted. I told the girl I'd wear them and paid her. She put my shoes in a box for me, and I walked out.

I walked up Lake toward Colorado, and I noticed people noticing my boots. I felt really classy. I felt great. I thought about buying some fabric so I could make a dress that would compliment my new boots, and when I reached Colorado I turned left and walked in the direction of the good fabric stores. I went into Vera's first, but I didn't see anything I could use, and I continued in the direction of Maxine's. I was almost there when I stopped and drew back into the entrance of a shoe store. Up ahead was Darrell, his face stark against the darkness of a tinted window. He was absorbed in looking at something, either his reflection or the watches in the window. He moved slowly along, coming towards me. He looked away for a moment, and in that moment I made myself scarce.

I backed into the shoe store. There was one customer, a tiny grey-haired lady in a nubbly pink coat, and one salesman, a skinny guy in a screaming plaid jacket. They were involved with the tennis shoes.

I turned to the dress shoe section and kept my back to the window. The shoes were terrible, cheap leather and plastic. I picked up one number with a spike heel and patent leather bow, and ventured a glance out the window. Darrell seemed to be gone. I wanted to be sure. I made my way along the display shelves, absently picking up shoes and putting them down again, moving closer to the old lady and the salesman.

The old lady was holding a blue tennis shoe up to the salesman's face and gesturing with it. The salesman looked tired.

"You don't understand, young man. I want this shoe in black. Not that one. This one."

"I know Ma'am, but we don't carry that style in black. If you want a black tennis shoe, you can try this other style. Otherwise, I can't help you."

I caught a glimpse of her face as I passed them. She was squinting up at him as though she believed he was lying and she meant to interrogate him until he broke.

I approached the door and cautiously looked around. Darrell was gone, so I stepped out into the sunlight again.

At Maxine's I found a beautiful cotton knit and a suitable pattern for it. I looked at some shirt patterns and thought about making something for Gary, but I thought the better of it. Maybe later, if things worked out.

I daydreamed all the way back along Colorado and down Lake and stopped for coffee at a sidewalk cafe. The cafe was half empty, so I didn't feel crowded. I set my packages down by the base of the table and stretched out my legs so I could look at my boots again. I was contemplating them when the waiter appeared, looking very serious. He jotted down my order and disappeared. I sat up and crossed my legs. I wondered what Gary was up to. I hadn't seen him for four days. The thought of him making love to another woman made my stomach clench, so I tried to talk myself out of believing it. I reminded myself that I was paranoid, that he was very busy with his own projects and I with mine, that I should be more trusting. I still felt nervous. The waiter returned with my coffee and retreated before I could say anything to him.

When I arrived at school there were forty-five minutes left before class, so I joined the crowd by the mirror pools. The area was mobbed since it was the first sunny day after a series of rainy days. The grass was still too damp to sit on, so the concrete walls of the pools were lined with students, and the benches were full. There were even people sitting on the walkways. I found a place on a bench under a tree and schemed on a sunnier spot occupied by a girl who was eating a bag lunch, reading from a philosophy textbook and glancing up occasionally to watch the frisbee players. An Irish setter galloped by, scattering small birds. The setter made a beeline for the frisbee through the far mirror pool, sending out sparkling plumes of water as he plunged across, and a line of people abandoned their seats on the edge of the pool to avoid getting wet. The girl with the philosophy book smiled. Sprinting across the lawn, the boys with the frisbee called the dog and lured him away from the water. They threw the frisbee and it soared in an arc as the wind caught it; it rode up the face of the wind and then dropped. The dog danced in anticipation, his red coat shimmering in the sunlight. He lunged up to catch the frisbee and the impact of it made him stagger back slightly. The boys applauded.

The best thing about my new boots was not the color, which I loved, or the fit, which was fine, but the texture of the leather. It was intriguingly soft. As I watched the boys with the frisbee and the dog and the girl, I found myself reaching down to touch the leather of my boot. I wondered if anybody noticed. The gesture did seem a little bit masturbatory. I was suddenly conscious that someone might be watching me. The girl was working on an apple, lost in the intricacies of being dainty; the people on the walkways and the benches were conversing or reading or watching the antics of the dog and the frisbee players. Except one. Over on the broad front steps of Smith building, on the very top steps, out of the sun, slouched a familiar and unwelcome figure. He was too far away to know for sure that I had seen him; he could only know that my face had turned briefly in his direction. But I knew he was watching me. I looked away. Should I leave? Should I let him drive me away? No. I heard the girl close her book and saw her stand up. As she walked away, I slid over to where she had been sitting and felt the sun begin to warm me. I closed my eyes and shut out everything but the warmth.

I sat that way for quite a while, feeling the sun shifting on my face as the wind moved the branches of the tree, and feeling the wind. It was a pleasant combination of cool and warm. There was a great confusion of sound which I found soothing. But there was also a point of irritation I could not forget; I was being watched.

"Excuse me." he said.

I opened my eyes.

"May I sit down?" he asked.

I said yes; yes, of course, and he sat at a discreet distance. I shaded my eyes and looked away.

"You've been avoiding me." he said suddenly.

I glanced at him, saw the pale, worried face, dark hair swept back from forehead by the wind, blue windbreaker open and flapping, grey sweatshirt bunched under his chin.

"What makes you think so?"

"Why won't you talk to me?"

I put my hands over my face to clear my eyes and tried to think of a way to handle this. I took my hands away and looked toward the mirror pools. One of the boys from drawing class was off to the far side of the far mirror pool, setting something carefully in the water.

"Why are you avoiding me?"

"I'm not." I said. "I'm always on the run and I've got a thousand things to think about, so I might seem to be avoiding you when I'm not."

"But it's making me miserable. I can't eat, I have trouble sleeping. When I feel like this I go out and get drunk."

Spots of sun sliding over his face. He's angry. The boy is still leaning over the water, positioning something; he takes his hand away. A boat.

"Have you ever noticed that I was drinking?"

"You shouldn't, Darrell. Not because of me. Don't you have a girlfriend? How can you get so upset over me when we hardly know each other?"

I am beginning to feel cold. The shade is moving to my right as the sun changes. I wonder if the grass is dry enough to sit on yet. How pleasant it would be to stretch out in the sun.

"We could work on our relationship. We could have it any way you like."

Relationship? What relationship? The boy has straightened up to see what the boat will do. The water is choppy and the boat is moving sideways. The water is so bright that the boat is almost impossible to see. I shade my eyes.

"Wouldn't you be willing to try?"

"But I already have a relationship with somebody."

Gary. And what is Gary doing right at this moment? Will he try to call me? Wish he would. If he could just slow down for a few hours, make love to me, be warm together. I watch the boat veer away from the edge of the pool. The setter is romping in the water again, making big waves for the little boat. Darrell is silent for a moment. I feel dazed. The water is so bright that my eyes hurt if I look at it for any length of time; I want to close my eyes, but Darrell needs to feel that I am paying attention.

"I don't have to be the main guy in your life."

His mouth makes a sticking sound as he talks. I wish he would go get a drink of water, excuse himself and go, but he stays. The boy moves slowly alongside the mirror pool, encouraging, and sometimes for an instant I see a flash of sail before it disappears again in the brilliance of the water. My eyes ache. I am leaning away from Darrell when I feel him grip my arm. I haven't been listening. I turn to him; sun rakes my vision. He releases me and stands. He looks so confused and lost that I don't know what to say or do, and before I can recover he is gone.

✳

On Tuesday morning Darrell wasn't at photography lecture, so I put him out of my mind and thought about work. The instructor told us that he had a project in mind. He wanted us to do a series of family portraits, but he didn't want them to look like the ones you see in the shop windows of professional photographers. He said he wanted to see some imagination at work, and then he turned us loose. At first I was a little worried because I didn't have much of a family to work with, but after conferring with my classmates I began to be enthusiastic. There was one redheaded, chubby guy named Jack whose family was in Minnesota. He lived with Keith, another redhead, Keith's sister, Marta, and an assortment of gay men. And a duck. The duck's name was America, and

Jack sometimes brought her to school. America wasn't with him at the moment because he was afraid someone might step on her in the darkroom. I had seen her following at his heels as he walked across the quad, and I had liked him right off. So I sat and listened to Jack go into ecstasies over the possibilities of family portraits. After a while I interrupted to ask what one could do with a speed-freak brother and an alcoholic mother.

"Let's see . . . needles and bottles . . . got any animals?" he asked.

"No."

"Maybe I could set you up with one. Want a puppy?"

The next day Jack brought me a puppy that looked mostly like a cocker spaniel. Keith turned it over and looked and declared it a girl. Jack suggested that I do a series of baby pictures. We put the puppy on the floor, and it wandered off, nose to the ground, while we tried to think of a name for it. We couldn't think of anything that sounded quite right, so we called her Dog.

I made a trip to a toy store downtown and bought some props. I bought some frames, too. They actually had pink and blue frames for baby pictures, so I bought some in different sizes. When I got back to the photography lab, Keith was feeding Dog bits of hamburger. He helped me set her up. We blocked off a corner of the lab and set up a paper backdrop. In front of that we set a short stool with a baby blanket draped over it, and we put Dog on the stool. Keith held her while I tied a baby bonnet on her head. I set a pacifier by her paws. We started out with the camera on a tripod and got some good straight shots; Keith tempted Dog with hamburger so that she would be looking up eagerly and smiling. Then I tried some hand-held shots. Dog got bored, stood up, looked around, and jumped off the stool. I kept taking pictures. I photographed her retreat until she was out of range under a table. I was still on my hands and knees when Jack came over to me with some prints and told me to look at them one at a time, in order.

The first was a straightforward group photograph; a row of people standing, a row of people seated in front of them in chairs, and a row of people seated on the floor at the feet of the people in the chairs. And the duck. I recognized Marta sitting on the floor, and Keith and Jack seated in chairs; a couple of the other men had familiar faces. The only odd thing about the picture was the fact that the duck had a child's jacket buttoned around it. Everyone else was wearing pants. Jack informed me that this was his family and that all of these people lived in his house from time to time.

In the second picture the people were grouped as in the first, but everyone was wearing dresses, including the duck.

"Not bad." said Jack from over my shoulder.

The third picture was the same, except that there wasn't an article of clothing anywhere to be seen.

The fourth picture was the same as the third, except that it was taken from the rear.

We trooped off down the hall, Keith and Jack and me, with our cameras slung over our shoulders, Dog in my bag. The sun on the quad was dazzling, and as we stepped out of the Smith building into the warmth Jack did a little dance yelling, "Hooray for summer in winter!" On our way across the quad we picked up more friends; one of the men from Jack's house joined us, and we found Marta and her boyfriend sunning themselves. Marta yawned and stretched and looked beautiful, and she and her boyfriend tagged along after us. Jack saw some cheerleaders and yelled "Yahoo!" at them, and then we stepped into the cafeteria.

We grabbed a table by the window that faced out over the quad. I went over and got into line in the food service area. Gary and Dan were standing over by the donuts, sipping coffee. Dan looked at me, and then Gary followed his glance, saw me and waved. I waved back. The lady behind the counter asked me what I'd like, and I said blueberry yogurt even though I didn't really want it, and she handed me a carton. Then I went to the coffee machine and punched the button for coffee with cream and sugar, and Gary was standing next to me.

"What have you been up to?" he asked very casually, like a friend who hadn't seen me for months.

"Oh, taking pictures and stuff. I got a dog." And I showed him Dog curled up asleep in the bottom of my bag. I felt like punching him out.

"Why don't we get together tonight? Got anything planned?"

I ignored his question and tried to get Dan's attention instead. He was wandering off toward the cashier, so I called, "Hey, Dan! Come here a sec! I've got to make an appointment to take some pictures of you and Mom together!" He nodded and pointed to a table and got in line at the cashier's desk.

"You want to go to a movie?"

"What movie?"

"There's a couple of Warhol movies on Sunset, or we could see some W. C. Fields movies."

I tasted my coffee and thought about it. "What time?"

"I'll pick you up at six and we can go get something to eat."

I went over to Dan's table and explained my project to him while Gary sat in silence. Dan kind of liked the idea and agreed to a sitting, so I told him I'd work it out with Mom and let him know the day and the hour.

By the time I had finished talking to Gary and Dan, my friends had settled themselves around their table. I pulled up a chair and arranged my bag in my lap carefully so Dog would not be disturbed. The sun was coming in the window like mad. Actually, the sun was coming through the walls, being as the walls were only glass. The cafeteria was a cube of glass held together by metal trim, and it offered a view of expanses of concrete bordered by succulents and an occasional sapling. Jack was pretending that the quad was a giant shooting gallery.

"Keith! Quick! How many points? Quick before he gets out of range!"

Keith was keeping score. Marta was selecting targets. I formed a telescope with my hands and peered through it, looking for victims. I found a cheerleader, and Jack scored fifteen points, explaining that anything in a uniform was worth five extra points.

I started doing my telescope again. Darrell stepped right into range.

"Oh shit." I said.

"How many points?" asked Jack.

"I don't know. Do you get extra points for a psychotic?"

"Naw, they're so common."

"Ten points."

And Jack shot him down. But he kept coming, hesitating, looking around, fingering his camera.

6.

I went home around two so I could finish up my knit dress and wear it to the movies that night. My machine was set up on my desk, and parts of the dress were scattered on the couch, over the chairs, and on the floor. I turned on the radio and sewed, and I had that dress finished by five. I tried it on, and I swear I almost looked like a model. But I didn't have time to mess around in front of the mirror. I took a bath and washed my hair, and while I was putting on the finishing touches, Gary knocked on the door. I let him in and went back to brushing my hair.

"Nice dress." Gary said to my back.

I looked at him in the mirror.

"Want to smoke a joint?"

"Sure."

Gary lit up and took a hit, handed me the joint, and then spread himself out on the couch. I handed the joint back to him and he stuck it in his mouth. He picked up some pictures that were lying on the table.

"Those are old." I said.

He inhaled, handed me the joint, said nothing. I stuck my head in the closet, looking for my coat, and Gary looked silently at my photographs. I hated that.

"Okay." I said, putting on my coat.

"What's the hurry? Let's finish this smoke."

He stayed on the couch, and I remained standing in my coat as we passed the joint back and forth. Dog woke up and wandered sleepily over to Gary, who blew smoke in her face.

He took me to a Mexican restaurant deep in Pasadena. I was glad we went there because the people didn't care what you looked like, and they didn't care if you were a little high, as long as you were quiet, and besides the food was good. We took a table for two under a bright mural of Mexican peasants dancing. Fortunately it was a weeknight and the place wasn't packed; the dope was strong and I felt a little nervous. I wanted to have something alcoholic to relax me. I took a chance when the waitress came and ordered a beer. She didn't even look twice at me. I drank the beer as fast as I could, and it helped a little. Gary and I didn't talk much, and I was glad when the food arrived because it was an excuse not to talk at all. Gary kept looking at me with an expression I couldn't read. It pissed me off, so I looked right back at him with the blankest expression I could maintain. I wanted to ask him what his story was, but he beat me to it.

"What's with you tonight?"

"What?"

"Why do you keep staring at me like that?"

"Is it making you nervous?"

He ignored the question.

"What have you been doing that makes you so fucking bitchy?"

"What have I been doing?" What have you been doing?"

"What?"

"Like where have you been every night for the last week?"

I kept my hands in my lap because they were trembling. Gary looked as graceful and poised as a snake. His voice was absolutely smooth.

"I don't have to report to you."

The waitress appeared and asked if we wanted anything else. I ordered another beer, and she took my half-eaten tostada away. Gary lit a cigarette and leaned his elbows on the table as he smoked. I looked him right in the eye.

"Why do you spend time with me at all if you've got something else going?"

"We're friends, remember?"

He took another drag on his cigarette, and then he stuck the cigarette in his mouth and squinted at me through the smoke. I reached over the table and plucked the cigarette out of his mouth and threw it on the floor.

"Don't make a scene." he said.

"Don't you know how to be anything other than a bastard?" I whispered to him.

The waitress set my beer in front of me and I poured half of it into my glass. My hands had stopped trembling and I felt incredibly calm. I sipped my beer, ignoring Gary. Gary had lit another cigarette and was quietly smoking. I didn't feel like talking to him anymore. So we sat in silence. I finished what was in my glass and stood up. I took my jacket off its hook.

"Where do you think you're going?" Gary asked.

As an afterthought I opened my purse and tossed a couple of bills on the table. Then I walked out of the restaurant without looking back at Gary. I walked about half a mile and started hitchhiking home. Naturally a kid with bad acne scars picked me up in his hot Ford. I lit up a cigarette with the intention of sticking it in his face if he tried anything, but I think he got the idea just by my attitude and didn't try anything more than to ask where I went to school. I made him let me out several blocks from my house and I didn't walk directly home. I stood outside a sporting goods store and looked at the baseball shirts.

Two big tears slid down my face and dropped off my chin. I stayed in front of the sporting goods store because I didn't want to walk blindly down the street crying. At first my thoughts and feelings were flying all over the place, but they settled into a big lonely lump in the pit of my stomach. I was just getting myself under control when I became conscious of a man slowly walking by me for the third time in two minutes. He noticed me noticing him and took it as a signal to approach.

"Excuse me." he said, peering into my face.

"Get out of here." I said.

"Listen, why don't we go have a cup of coffee?" he persisted, trying to stand directly in front of me. I backed away from him.

"If you don't get out of here fast I'm going to scream." I said still backing.

"What's your name?" he continued, as if he hadn't heard a word I'd said. Maybe he hadn't heard. He acted as though someone had wound him up and pointed him in my direction and he didn't have any choice in the matter and no way to understand. I turned around and ran.

By the time I got home, I had decided that my night would not be completely ruined. I didn't want to be at home alone because I could do nothing there to get my mind off

Gary. I wanted work. So as fast as I could, I changed into jeans and a tee shirt and headed for school.

But the lab was mobbed. I'd never tried to work in the darkroom during night classes, and I hadn't realized that it would be so busy. My haven was full of housewives and plumbers and secretaries who monopolized the enlargers. In spite of them I pushed my sleeves up to my elbows and started to work developing my baby pictures. The negatives looked promising. I managed to get one of the enlargers to myself and started printing some five by seven portraits. The pictures had just the right effect; they were traditionally baby-cute, just exactly the kind of pictures Mom and Dad proudly displayed on the mantle. By nine forty-five I was on my third print, and I turned to the lady next to me to ask how much longer the lab would be open. Before she had a chance to answer, a male voice said, "We have to have everything cleaned up and be out by ten-fifteen."

I turned to Darrell, who was standing behind me, a tray of wet prints in his hands.

"Thank you." I said, and I smiled at him. I had no idea how long he'd been in the lab. He waited as though he were expecting something, smiling a very tentative smile. I excused myself and walked around him to the fixer trays. Once my print was floating in the fixer I looked up again, and he was still staring at me. But he wasn't smiling. He looked really bad, and I remembered what he'd said about drinking. He sure didn't look like he was taking very good care of himself, but no matter how I tried I couldn't feel sympathetic. He turned away.

I made up my mind to ignore him completely, no matter what. I packed up my things, put my final print in the dryer, and walked purposefully out the door. As I walked to the parking lot, I had the creepy feeling that I was being followed, but I would not turn to look.

7.

Thursday afternoon when I was supposed to be in drawing class, which I was flunking for nonattendance, I was sneaking down a hall in Smith building. My object was to get within range of a couple I had been observing. They were having a very cool discussion. The girl, who was pretty in a superficial sort of way, seemed to be trying to get rid of the guy, who apparently thought she was just playing hard to get and continued to talk as though he were having some success. She was obviously getting impatient, though she didn't want to be rude. It looked interesting, and I hoped to catch some good pictures. I was within six feet of them and focusing on her face when I felt someone grab my arm, and I was backed up against the wall, face to face with Darrell.

"Why won't you talk to me?" he demanded in a shallow voice, as though he couldn't get any air. He saw that I was about to say something, anything, so he gasped, "Don't lie to me!"

He was pinning me to the wall with both hands, not hurting me, but preventing any move on my part. I didn't know what to say, and I was afraid to look away from him, so I just gazed into his face and listened to him struggle for air. I thought he would kill me if I didn't respect his emotion. Apparently the people passing by thought we were lovers arguing, or else thought nothing at all; nobody seemed to notice us.

"Look, we should go somewhere quiet and talk." I said. I felt him relax a little.

"Where?"

"My apartment?"

He slumped on my bed; I sat on my desk.

"Look," he said, "There are possibilities." He glanced up to see if I understood. I didn't.

"We don't necessarily have to be lovers." he explained. "We could have a more or less platonic relationship. If you would spend a certain amount of time with me, that would be enough. I would like something more, you understand, but your friendship would be enough for now."

"But Darrell . . ."

"No, wait. Don't think you're all that important. You're not. You only rank sixth on my list."

"Your list?"

I wanted to give him water because his mouth was sticking again as he talked.

"Yes, I know other girls. The most important one was Janet, she's in San Francisco now, she was the one I wanted most. She had the figure and the face. We used to talk. We used to talk about all the things I was interested in. She liked politics. She married a guy I'd never met, and I bet it won't last. Married at eighteen."

The mouth was still sticking badly.

"Oh, the next one, Kathy, she was nice. Not as pretty as Janet, but more kind. Intelligent, too. But she went and got pregnant by someone else. And Susan, who wanted to be a nurse; we had a long talk one evening on her porch. Every time I tried to tell her how I felt, she changed the subject. Marie was involved with someone else when I met her, so I never had a chance." He tried to swallow and his throat made a clicking sound. "She had the prettiest hair. Karen I still see every time I go home. She says she's depressed, but she can't explain it, so she is distant."

He paused for a moment.

"The greatest possibilities are with you," he said, without looking up.

"Me?"

"The eyes are the right color. And your hair is just the kind I like best. You've got high cheekbones, that's good, and your build is perfect except for your breasts. If they could be just a little bit bigger." He hesitated. "Look, I don't need to go to bed with you, although I want that. I don't need to see you a lot, although that would be wonderful. But I do need your friendship."

He sat with his eyes downcast and tried to swallow again, and again his throat clicked dry. I watched him run his tongue around the inside of his mouth with effort.

"I need a drink of water." he said.

I went to the sink and filled a glass for him. He accepted the water without looking at me and drank it down. I could see that it didn't help at all, but he didn't ask for more. We sat in silence for a few minutes while he tried to get control of himself and I tried to think of some way out. The sun was going down, lighting up the room, lighting up dust motes so that the air seemed clogged with them.

"Do you find me repulsive?" he asked.

I glanced at the sunken chest, the flabby skin. Then I looked him in the eye and said, "No. No, you are not repulsive. But, Darrell, we can't have this relationship you talk about. We can't have any relationship."

"What? Why not?" he demanded, his face twitching, slipping out of control.

I stared at him, fascinated, deciding whether to tell him the truth. He stared back, eyes gone rigid, face twisting. Somewhere in my brain a warning flashed, something about that impulse which was forcing his eyes back on mine. For a moment we were locked into each other, and I think he almost understood. Then he asked again.

"Tell me why not."

"Because I don't want to take on the responsibility of caring for you."

"Don't want to take on the responsibility? Then why did you ever bother to talk to me?" His voice rose hysterically. "Why did you talk to me until four in the morning?"

"It was an accident. You were there and I needed someone to talk to."

"I thought you cared about me as a person."

"I do care, but I don't want to hang around with you."

He forced air out of his lungs as though he were finding it hard to breathe, as though he were about to collapse.

"Darrell, how old are you?"

"Twenty-one."

"And have you ever made love to a woman?"

He looked up, and his eyes were full of tears.

"No."

It was the wrong question. I tried again.

"Hey, I don't know how to explain it to you. My time is important to me, that's why I'm not going to waste it with Gary anymore, that's why I'm not going to pretend I want to be with you. It isn't that I don't care, I just. . . ."

I should have recognized his distress.

I heard him sob once, saw him rush out the door. I sat for a moment, startled, then followed. He was gone. In the time it took me to reach the landing, he had escaped.

8.

I looked for Darrell. On Friday I went to the registrar's office and asked one of the ladies behind the desk for his address. I remember how strange I felt. The Santa Ana winds had come up in the night, desert winds bringing desert heat, and everyone was dazed and dressed for summer, hair gone electric and sticking to faces. I was haunted by the hot-cold feeling of air against skin and skin against skin. For the first time since I left Gary, I felt sexual, and alone. In the office I was shy and aware of all the bare arms, bare legs, and the air conditioning, newly activated, raising goosebumps on my arms. I asked a thickset lady in a blue dress if she would look up some information for me, and for a moment I was afraid she would refuse or demand a reason I wouldn't be able to give, but she was preoccupied, too; she asked only that I spell the name. I guessed at it. She wrote it down on a slip of paper, SCHLEYER, and went away to another room. I waited, feeling like a thief.

She came back, walking as though her feet hurt, staring at the piece of paper. She handed it to me. I looked at it without seeing what was written, folded the paper and put it in my pocket.

"Need anything else?" she asked, gazing out the window behind me.

"Is he still registered?" I asked stupidly.

"He's officially registered or his name wouldn't be in the file."

"Thanks." I said.

I went outside and thought about it. Find him and apologize? No, let him calm down. I've never seen a man so upset in quite that way. Would he try. He was desperate.

My fingers creased the paper in my pocket.

He has no right. How can he make such a demand on me?

I took the paper out and looked at the address. Marengo Avenue. I put it back.

I went to class and waited while everyone settled down. Waited through the lecture, turning to look each time the door opened. When, after lecture, he still hadn't shown, I postponed my work and went for a walk. The heat was wonderful dry heat, light upon the skin, easy on the spirit. He couldn't stay depressed in this weather. Could anyone? I walked all over campus, crossing my path once or twice; I walked to the cafeteria and bought iced tea. I sat outside on the steps in the shade and watched people come and go, and when I had finished my tea, I dumped the ice on my toes and watched it melt.

He'll find me, I thought.

But he didn't find me on Friday, nor did he find me Saturday.

By Sunday the wind and heat were beginning to chafe. Too much skin, an unnatural season. It wasn't right, this game of hiding; it was taking me away from what I wanted to do. My thoughts eddied away. I looked up SCHLEYER in the phone book. No number.

Did he mean it? I went for a walk. I walked across town, irritated by the static in my hair, irritated and lonely. I tried to concentrate. If he were going to disappear, where would he go? Did he know anyone? Were there relatives? I stopped at a gas station and shut myself in the phone booth. No Schleyers. Nothing near. I walked down Colorado to a delicatessen and bought a coke, walked into an alley to drink it, alone.

If he had killed himself, wouldn't someone know it by now?

I could ask his landlady.

But I didn't want to know.

I walked back out on the sidewalk and found a trash can to throw the empty bottle in, and then cruised along the store windows, watching my legs as I walked.

Had I teased him?

No.

But I hadn't gone more than two days in a row without seeing him, since the beginning, and this made three. Surely he would turn up downtown. Perhaps he hid in the darkness of one of those bars, out of the heat, out of the sun, away from the screaming of all that skin. He would come out eventually, and it made no sense to be walking up and down, waiting.

I made an appointment with myself. Monday I would go to the photography lab. If he didn't show, I would find him.

Monday came and went without him. I waited around the photography lab for three hours, telling myself that if I left I would miss him, make an unnecessary trip to his apartment and further complicate things. I had myself almost convinced that he was just hiding and that he would show up soon. But that night I couldn't get him off my mind as I tried to fall asleep. I visualized his body, dead. I tried to guess what method of suicide he would prefer. My hands went clammy when I thought about it. The next morning I went to my dresser and found the scrap of paper with his address pencilled on it, looked at it once again, folded it into my pocket. I was unlocking the car door when a thought occurred to me; what if he should recognize my car and disappear again before I had a chance to talk to him? I would take the bus.

The bus hurtled downtown and I slouched, trying to keep my legs free so they wouldn't sweat and stick to the seat. I kept my hand deep in my pocket so I could touch the paper with the address on it. We raced toward Marengo Avenue. I barely had time to reach up and pull the bell-cord and we were upon it. A wino watched me step off the bus and started to say something, but I walked resolutely by and took the paper out of my pocket. 613 Apt. C. The business district extended only a few blocks, giving way to shabby houses that had been broken up into apartments, and on every available porch and stairway people sat, dressed in summer clothes. They watched me walk by.

The street broadened after another block or two, and I walked under dusty old trees. The six-hundred block was lined with unkempt Victorians gone grey with age. 613 had been painted green, but the paint was peeling away. I walked up the drive, into the entry, up a flight of stairs, and down the hall, and knocked on the door marked C. No answer. I knocked louder and waited. Nothing. I put my ear against the door and strained to hear something, anything. Nothing. I stood for a moment and wondered what to do. I couldn't just go away; I had to find out what was up.

So I stepped across the hall and knocked on that door. No answer. I moved down the hall and knocked at the next door. No answer. At the next door I could hear the sound of a TV, but nobody answered to my knock. I went downstairs and knocked at the manager's apartment and the door opened immediately. A woman about my mother's age frowned at me.

"What do you want?"

"I want to inquire about one of your tenants."

"Well, what?"

"Have you seen Darrell?"

"Who?"

"Darrell Schleyer."

"The tenants' business is none of my business." she snapped.

"Well I'm not trying to be nosy, but I'm worried about him. I have reason to believe he might be suicidal. I usually see him nearly every day, but I haven't seem him since Thursday, and the last time I saw him, he was very upset. So I just wanted to know if anybody had seen him. I just want to know if he's okay."

My heart was jumping all over the place, and she was scrutinizing my face.

"Have you seen him?" I asked again.

"No, but then I hardly ever see him." she said, and started to close the door.

"No, wait!" I said, and she stopped.

"Now what do you want?"

"Couldn't you at least let me see if he's there?"

"Listen here, it isn't legal to let just anybody go snooping around a tenant's premises."

"But what if he's hurt? Or dead? He could be lying in there right now."

She stared hard at me.

"You'd better not be playing games with me, young lady."

I shook my head.

"All right, we'll go see if he's there."

"Thank you."

She marched up the stairs and I followed her as quietly as I could. I waited behind her as she unlocked the door and stepped inside.

"Nobody here." she said.

"May I look?"

She stood by the door as I walked in. There was one large room, a tiny bathroom and a kitchenette. The place was a mess. It looked as though he hadn't spent much time there. He had made no effort to decorate the walls; there was not one picture, not even a poster. His furnishings consisted of one unmade bed, a dresser painted brown, a metal table and two unmatched chairs. The closet door was open, rumpled clothes strewn about it. No books, but a mound of newspapers in one corner. I checked the kitchenette and found dirty dishes in the sink. No Darrell. I tried the bathroom. He had smashed the mirror on the medicine cabinet, and the sink was full of broken, silvery glass.

"He's not here." I announced from the bathroom door.

The landlady shrugged.

I went to the side window and looked out. The window was dirty and the view of telephone wires and shrubs had the grainy quality of a bad photograph.

"Seen enough?" she asked.

"Thank you." I said.

"The tenants' business is none of my business," she repeated as she locked the door.

PART TWO

PASADENA, CALIFORNIA
FEBRUARY 16, 1974

I was born in Chicago in 1953. June 23, 1953 to be exact. I don't remember Chicago because when I was a few months old my parents moved to Los Angeles.

My father was an electrical engineer. He died a couple of years ago of cancer. My mother remarried to a man I didn't like. She wouldn't listen when I told her he was no good. I told her that she had to choose between him or me. She chose him, so I don't see her anymore.

I am a student. I study political science. I go to a junior college, but only because I cannot afford tuition at a university right now. I am living on savings and a little bit of money my dad left me. This summer I will work and save towards going to the university. I imagine that someday I will teach, or perhaps I will become a lawyer. Because I don't want to be a narrow person, I am also studying photography. I am not very good at it.

What I want to talk about is this girl, Melissa. Melissa O'Brien.

I met her at school in late January. January 22, 1974, to be exact. A Tuesday. I am in love with her.

Classes started for the Spring semester during the second week of January. The first session I took a seat in the back of the lecture room. I did that so that I could see everybody else, but they wouldn't see me. I didn't feel comfortable exactly being there, because I'm personally not very good at doing artistic things. I'm better at theory. There were maybe thirty people in the room, plus the professor. I noticed Melissa right away. She had long, thick hair, kind of blond. She was tall and slender. She was wearing tight blue jeans, new ones, and a red sweater that made her look all bundled up. I thought she was pretty. Melissa was one of maybe four other girls in the class.

The class met three times a week for lecture, critique and lab. It was a beginner's photography class, but most of the people in it seemed to be taking it pretty seriously. Melissa did. She was in there more than three times a week. She used the lab even when we weren't supposed to be there because other classes needed to use it, but Mr. Cheseborough, the teacher, tolerated extra people in the lab if they were serious about what they were doing.

During the first sessions, Mr. Cheseborough taught us the basics about shutter speed, lighting, and that kind of thing, and he gave us assignments. I couldn't afford to buy a camera, so I used a Nikon that belonged to the school. I wasn't comfortable using it at first, but after I saw my first contact sheet I started to feel better about it. As it turned out, I liked it, actually much more than I would have thought.

I didn't speak to Melissa until she spoke to me first. I hadn't really hoped to have any kind of relationship with her, but she changed all of that.

I met her by accident downtown one night, as I said, in late January. I had gone out for some dinner, and then I had gone to a bar for a beer. I was on my way home, walking down Colorado Boulevard, when I saw Melissa walking in my direction. She didn't see me at first. Even then, even before I had spoken with her, I had feelings for her because I had watched her in photography class. I knew she was special.

She was walking with her head down, kicking at little things on the sidewalk, and stopping every now and then to look in a window at a display. I walked by her and started to say hello, but she didn't even notice me then. I thought that I should just keep walking towards my place, I knew it wouldn't be right to follow her, but I knew she hadn't seen me and maybe she wouldn't notice if I did follow her for a while. So I walked for maybe another thirty feet or so, and then I stopped as if to look at some things in the window of a sporting goods store. I looked to see if she had noticed me yet. She hadn't. She moved on to another window, and I followed, looking into the window of a shoe store. And then she moved again and I moved in front of a used book store. This went on as we moved down the block, and then she waved at me. My heart started to pound in the most awful way, because I had thought she hadn't seen me. Then I thought that maybe she was waving at someone else behind me, so I looked, but nobody was there. When I looked at her again, she was crossing the intersection with her back to me, so I hurried to cross, too, before the light could change. Then I thought that I would walk past her, just to see what would happen. I wasn't going to look at her as I passed because I thought that she might get nervous, but I looked anyway, and she glanced at me as I was looking at her, and I felt my face getting hot and then she said hello to me. It was the first time she had ever spoken to me. I didn't know what to say.

She was very nice to me. She told me so many things about herself. She had had some trouble with the police and they had put her away for a while. She made a joke out of it, but it must have been terrible for her. She told me about the jobs she had had. She told me about her family. I think she had a hard life, but she joked about it, and she was really funny. I had to respect her for that, for being able to go through terrible experiences yet keep going and not be depressed about it. I told her about things that had happened to me, and I tried to make them funny, too. We walked as we talked. Then we came to her street. She told me that she lived up the hill. She started to walk up her street, and I wanted to go with her. I asked if it would be okay for me to walk her home. She said it was. She asked what time it was, and I told her. She said that it wasn't all that late, and would I like to have tea with her at her place? I was amazed that she would invite me to her house. I accepted.

I have never been so happy with a woman. We talked about everything. It was just so simple. She made tea, and we sat together at her table in her kitchen and we talked about our lives, how we felt about things. No woman had ever been that open with me about her life. We talked for more than six hours and it was wonderful. My feelings for her grew very deep that night.

When she saw me to the door, I wanted to kiss her, but of course I wouldn't dare. I had to get to know her better first. So I just made a comment about how late it was getting, and I told her what a wonderful time I'd had. I walked home, happier than I had been in years. I looked forward to seeing her again.

But the next day she wasn't in photography class. I was worried; maybe she had gotten sick? After lecture, I walked over to her apartment to see if she was okay. I went up the stairs and knocked on her door. Nobody answered, so I knocked again and put my ear up to the door, but I couldn't hear anything. Then I felt a little foolish, because maybe she had an appointment somewhere and couldn't come to class. I walked back to school for my afternoon classes. When I was done for the day, I decided not to go straight home, but to look for Melissa. She had said something about her brother doing a lot of work in the pottery lab, so I looked there first, but she wasn't there. I tried the darkroom, but she wasn't there, either. I wished I had gotten her phone number when I'd had the chance. I thought of the likeliest places where she might be and checked the cafeteria.

I walked up to the glass wall and looked into the dining area from the patio. It was difficult to see in clearly, because the outside light was fairly bright, so I cupped my hands around my eyes and got up next to the glass. I saw her. She was right in the middle of the cafeteria, sitting all alone at a table. She had her feet propped up on a chair, and she was drinking something with a straw, just like a little girl. She didn't see me at first, so I had a chance to observe her unawares. To me, she was beautiful. She really was like a little girl, with her hair down long like that. She was wearing pale colors, colors that looked good on her. She was wearing a fairly long, full skirt, but I could see her legs, because she had them up on the chair and the skirt was falling away from them. She had nice long legs. She had been daydreaming, but I think she saw me after a couple of minutes because she looked in my direction and then sat up suddenly and took her feet off the chair. But she didn't acknowledge me otherwise. I felt foolish all of a sudden, so I walked into the patio area and sat down at one of the picnic tables facing the cafeteria, so that maybe I would get a chance to say something to her if she walked out that way. I set my camera on the table in front of me.

I only had to wait a couple of minutes. I saw her get to her feet and pick up her bag. She walked to one of the trash bins and threw away her cup. I sat up. But she turned and walked toward the other door that led to the quadrangle instead of the patio, and she was out the door and down the stairs before I could catch her. She was too far away for me to get to her without running, and I didn't want to startle her, so I stayed back and walked far behind. She went into Smith Building, where the darkroom is.

I knew then that I would be able to talk to her, because I had a legitimate reason for being in the darkroom and she wouldn't think it was strange of me to strike up a conversation. I would talk to her about being with her the night before, and what that meant to me. But first I thought I should wait a little bit before following her into the lab, because I did not want to be too obvious. I sat down on a bench outside of Smith building and looked at my watch. When ten minutes had passed, I got up and walked down the stairs to the basement. My heart was pounding and my throat caught when I tried to swallow. I stopped in front of the door to the lab and concentrated for a moment, trying to slow my heart. I opened the door and went in. I found her standing at one of the chemical trays, making a print. She said hello when she heard me come in, but she was busy. I had planned to be casual, but my plans broke down when I saw her. I just stood there behind her while she worked. Finally she turned and looked at me, and said something about the talk we had had the night before. I had a rush of feeling then, and all I could say was that it had been a wonderful evening. I couldn't even look at her, because I was afraid of what she might see in my face. She was so special to me. I wanted to tell her over and over how much I loved her. Instead, I could not say anything.

She asked me what I was doing. I asked if she minded if I worked alongside her. She gave me a strange look, and I was afraid that I had alarmed her. She assured me that it would be okay, but then she did a terrible thing. She called me by the wrong name. I couldn't believe that she could have talked to me for such a long time and not have gotten my name right. I corrected her, and she kept talking to me, but I wasn't listening to the words because I was really amazed that she had gotten my name wrong. I wasn't sure what to think, and I watched her for a moment. Then she asked if she could see some of my pictures. That reassured me somewhat. I had been just about ready to walk away from her when she made that mistake about my name. But when she asked to see my pictures, all those feelings about her came back. I told her I would show her a contact sheet if she was really interested. She said that she was. I led her to the lockers and got a handful of contact sheets. While she waited I looked through them and picked out what I felt was the best. But I realized as I was looking at them that I was really not very good at taking pictures, not very good at all.

I watched the side of her face as she looked at the sheets. She was so pretty, so sure of herself. I wanted to touch her hair, but I could never, never make my hand do it. When she had looked through all the contact sheets, she began to ask questions about what I had been trying to do. She knew a lot technically about photography, and I learned from what she said. When I took the sheets back I asked her if she liked the pictures, or if she was just being kind. She said that she really liked them, and she actually picked out two or three and suggested that I print them in a particular way to get a certain effect. I agreed to do it. I felt much better than I had when I first walked into the lab. She really had a magic touch about her.

So I went to an enlarger and set it up, actually feeling happy. I was working in the lab with Melissa, and it was quiet except for the water trickling into the sink, and it was peaceful the way I felt it should be between us. But then I thought of a question to ask Melissa about my print, and when I turned to ask her she wasn't there. I looked all around the lab and saw that she had taken her things and left. I couldn't believe it. Everything had been going so well.

I couldn't continue working until I found out what had happened with her. I had to know how she felt about me. I was afraid that there might be a misunderstanding on her part, and I wanted to reassure her.

I put my things away in my locker and went looking for her. I tried the pottery studio again, but she wasn't there, and she wasn't in the cafeteria. I looked into all of the studios in Moline Building. I looked in all of the locker areas around the school. Then I decided to look through the parking lots for her car, to see if she had gone home. I found it after about half an hour of searching, in B Lot. I left her a note under the windshield wiper. I noticed that I could probably observe her car in the lot if I sat in the northwest corner of the cafeteria, right up next to the glass, so I went up the steps from the parking lot and went into the cafeteria and took that table. I got some coffee and sat there. I didn't have to wait very long. She showed up after about twenty minutes and took the note out from under the wiper. She stood looking at it for a moment. I realized that I was holding my breath and I let it out. Melissa folded my note and put it in her jacket pocket, unlocked her car, and got in. When she put her lights on, I couldn't see her clearly anymore. She drove away.

I had trouble sleeping that night. I could hear my land-lady's television downstairs. That didn't keep me awake, though. It was my feelings and my thoughts about Melissa that kept me awake. I wanted things clear between us. I wanted to come to some understanding about our relation-ship. I cared for her more than I had ever cared for anyone else, and I didn't want her to get away from me. I had to find some way to talk to her and explain how I felt. I wasn't sure how I could do that without upsetting her. I had cared about other women in the past, and some of them had not been able to understand or accept the depth of my feelings for them. Unfortunately, I tended to be very emotional sometimes when I tried to talk about those feelings, and misunderstandings arose. These thoughts and feelings went around and around my head. Eventually the landlady's TV was turned off, and the quiet nearly made me crazy. I got up and got my bottle of whiskey out of my desk drawer and sat down on my bed with it. I don't usually think about sex in any graphic way, but after drinking some of the whiskey I started to think about her that way. I thought about how I would have her physically. She would be standing there, and I would slowly take her clothes off of her. When she was naked I would lead her to the bed, and push her down on it. I would kiss her, but I wouldn't let her touch me, except maybe my face. I would pin her arms down by her side, or maybe above her head, and look at her that way, and kiss her, and kiss her breasts, holding her so she couldn't get away from me. She would be excited, and maybe trying a little bit to get away, but I would hold her down like that. Then I would make her undo my pants and take it out. Maybe she would suck on me, if I told her to. Maybe she would just touch it, very slowly and softly. Then I would go inside her, and I would do it to her until she started to yell, and then I would come. She would come, too. I would have her pinned again, her arms, I mean. I would only let her go long enough to take it out and maybe touch it a little. She would like it.

These thoughts excited me, so I did something about it. Afterwards, I drank some whiskey, hoping it would make me sleepy. It started to rain. I noticed it first when the wind blew some of the rain against my window. I looked at my clock then and saw that it was after three in the morning. After a while I went to sleep.

I woke up at ten the next morning, and it was raining heavily outside. My head felt terrible. I began thinking right away about Melissa, and how I could explain to her. I was trying to figure out how best to approach her. I put some coffee on and dressed quickly, because I didn't want to be late for class. The best thing would be just tell her straight out how I felt. Truth would be best. She seemed so evasive, though. I had to get her to stop for a little while and talk to me. I drank my coffee down too fast and it burned my mouth. I put on my rain things and took my camera and went outside. I hate the rain because I don't have a car, and when it rains I always get soaked and then I catch cold. I walked with my head down, trying to keep the wet out of my face, but the wind was blowing, and the rain blew down my neck and wet my shirt. I started to run, but I couldn't run more than half a block. By the time I got to school I was thoroughly cold and wet. As luck would have it, I saw Melissa going into Smith Building. She stopped just inside the door and was shaking out her umbrella when I caught up to her. I said hello to her, and she looked up at me as though she didn't recognize me. I asked her if she had gotten my note, even though I knew she had. I wanted to test her to see if she was truthful. She said that she had gotten it, and added that she had felt sick, and that was her reason for leaving the lab so suddenly. She seemed genuinely concerned about me because of my note. All of a sudden I didn't mind being wet and cold. She made all the difference.

We walked to class together, just the two of us. I wanted to tell her everything right then, because I was so full of feeling for her. But she seemed disturbed about something, and the hallway was too noisy for her to hear much of what I was saying. I was trying to make small talk about the assignment we were working on for photography class, and she kept having to ask me to repeat myself. It simply wasn't the right time. We were getting close to the lecture room, and I knew that once we were inside, I would lose her for the time being. So I felt that I had to make my move before we went in. I asked her right out if we could have another one of those long talks again. She didn't look at me directly. I could sense that something was very wrong, because I was willing her to look at me with all of my might, but she just wouldn't look. I didn't know what to do, because we kept moving steadily toward the classroom door, and yet she hadn't answered me. I had to have an answer. I just had to know. We arrived at the lecture room, and I opened the door, almost without feeling myself doing it. She passed through the door. She took a seat, and without asking her, I took the seat next to her. I watched her through the the entire lecture, telling myself the whole time to stop, but not being able to stop. I made her uncomfortable, and I knew that I was doing it, but I couldn't help myself. So I wasn't really surprised when she left before the lecture had ended. She said that she had an appointment, but I could see by her expression that she didn't. I couldn't be angry at her for lying, though, because it was all my fault. I hadn't handled the situation well. I would have to try again.

The weekend was hell. If she was trying to avoid me, she succeeded. I didn't see her for three days. I thought I would see her at school on Friday, but she wasn't around. I kept checking back at the darkroom but she never showed up. I spent the whole day making the rounds of all the places she could possibly be on campus: the darkroom, the drawing studios, the painting studios, the library, the pottery studio, the cafeteria. I walked by the lockers and checked all of the hallways. It rained all day. By the time I had figured out that she wasn't going to show up, it was late afternoon. Then I thought of calling her. I found a phone booth and looked in the telephone directory, but her number wasn't listed. I called directory assistance, but there wasn't anyone by the name of Melissa O'Brien listed. The school offices had closed at four o'clock, so I couldn't ask there. I thought of going to the pottery studio and looking for her brother, but I had never seen her brother and didn't know what he looked like. I was afraid that if I started asking around, I might arouse suspicions; it might get back to her that I had been looking for her. It was too much of a risk. On my way home from school I stopped by her place and knocked on her door. She wasn't home. I considered leaving a note for her, but my fear of further upsetting her stopped me. So I went back to my place. I couldn't stand to be alone, so I stayed home long enough to change into dry clothes, and then I went out again. There was an inexpensive Mexican place over on Fair Oaks near Colorado. I went there for dinner.

They served me a lot of food, and normally I would have eaten all of it. But that night I could hardly eat because of Melissa. I had a beer with my food, and then I had another one. The people who ran the restaurant never bothered people who sat for hours at a table, because the restaurant was never full. Sometimes, like that night, I was the only English-speaking person in the place, and all the time they played Mexican music on the jukebox. So I sat and had several beers, long after they had taken my plate away. I was seated facing the door, and I watched the rain come down, and then let up, and then come down again. I knew that Melissa must be out with some other guy. It was the first time that the thought had ever occurred to me. I had never seen her with any guys at school, and nothing she had said to me had ever made me think that she might have someone in her life. But this was a Friday night, and on Friday nights people went out together. So maybe that was why she was trying to avoid me. Maybe she had something going with some guy, maybe even a guy at school, and maybe she was afraid that if the guy saw her talking to me, it would mess things up between her and the guy. That would be a legitimate reason for her to act the way she acted toward me.

I thought about that for a while. Mentally I went back over every time I had seen her, and what she had been doing, and whether or not things would have happened as they did if she really were involved with someone else. For example, would she have been walking alone in the parking lot at night if she had a boyfriend at school? Wouldn't she sometimes be with her boyfriend in the cafeteria, having something to drink or eat and talking? Wouldn't I have seen them together? I reviewed all of the individuals I had seen her sitting with at any time. None of them had appeared to be her lover. None of them seemed the type of guy I would have imagined her with. She had never touched anybody, and I think that she would be a physically affectionate type of person with a boyfriend. I concluded that it wasn't likely that she was involved with someone at school. It wasn't really likely, either, that she had someone serious outside of school. She lived alone. She spent many of her evenings at school, as far as I could tell. But on the weekends she might be with someone, and I would never know unless I watched her apartment.

I considered that thought. If I watched her apartment, would anyone catch me at it? Would she see me? How could I go about it? I glanced around the restaurant to see if there were any newspapers around. There was one on a stool at the counter, and nobody was sitting near it. I went over and got it and looked at the classified ads. I looked in the rental section. I was looking for a room near her apartment, preferably on the same street as her place, same block if I could get it. There wasn't anything close enough to make it worth moving there. I tossed the paper on a chair. I couldn't just walk by her place frequently, because there was just too much of a risk that she would happen to look out her window and see me doing it. With the way things were going, she might be frightened.

I ordered another beer. I was starting to feel drunk. When I finished the beer, I paid my bill and left. It wasn't raining very hard. I stood in a doorway and waited for a bus to take me down Colorado to Melissa's street. I was drunk enough that I didn't mind the wet.

As I walked up the hill toward her place, I rehearsed what I would say if I should run into her. It was about eight o'clock. It was early enough that I could say that I had been in the neighborhood and that I was dropping by to see if she would like to see a movie, since the weather was so bad. That seemed normal enough. Maybe she would accept, and we could go see something, and then afterwards we could go out for something to drink, and then I could explain to her, when she was relaxed. A light was on in her apartment. I stood on the sidewalk and considered what that meant, and watched for shadows moving against the light. Nothing moved. Chances were that she had left a light on to discourage burglars. Chances were that she wasn't home. The rain began to come down harder, so I went up the walk and up the stairs and knocked on her door. She didn't answer, so I put my ear up to the door and held my breath and listened. There wasn't a sound inside. It had really started to pour, so I stood there outside her door for a good twenty minutes waiting for it to let up. Or at least that's what I would have told her if she had appeared; the truth was that I didn't give a damn about the rain or how hard it came down. I was waiting for her. When it did let up, I waited some more. After I had been there for about an hour I was too cold to stand there anymore, and I went back on the sidewalk to see if anything about the light inside her apartment had changed. Nothing had changed. I walked up and down the block a couple of times to see if there were any rooming houses, or any sheltered places where I could conceal myself and wait and observe her apartment. There really wasn't any place where I wouldn't be risking being seen and I didn't want anybody calling the police on me thinking that I was a prowler. The frustration actually brought tears to my eyes. If she only knew how I loved her, what I was willing to do for her.

I went back down the hill and walked for a couple of blocks along Colorado until I found a late-night coffee shop. I went in and took a booth by a window on the street so that I could watch for her car, and I ordered coffee and a piece of pie. It was about nine-thirty. I took a paperback out of my pocket and opened it and pretended to read, but I spent most of the time staring out the window in hopes of seeing her car. Of course I considered the possibility that if she were out with someone else, she might be in his car, and I wouldn't see her go by. Or possibly they might approach her place from another direction. Or they might even stay at his place for the night, and never even come back this way. I sat in the coffee-shop until eleven o'clock. Then I went out again and walked to her place to see if she was there. The lights were the same, and again she didn't answer the door. I spent another half-hour there. I considered leaving her a note, but my instincts warned against it. I went for a walk up the hill. I walked for a long time in neighborhoods where I had never been before. I told myself that I should be observant, because there might be something that I should come back to and photograph, but I was too preoccupied. I walked back to her place and got there at 1:30 in the morning. The lights still hadn't changed, and she wasn't there.

The rain woke me Saturday morning at about six. I could not go back to sleep. Normally on Saturdays I sleep as late as I can, and then go out for a late breakfast in a coffee shop. Then I do chores. I do my wash, and I study. I tried to read, since I couldn't sleep. It was no use. I got out of bed and took a hot shower, and then I fixed coffee and took my cup to my desk. I had decided when I was in the shower that I would write her a letter and deliver it to her by hand, or maybe slip it under her door and leave, so that there wouldn't be an uncomfortable scene. I hadn't decided how to handle that detail yet. I found my lined paper and wrote:

Dear Melissa:

I hope this is the least upsetting way
to do this (I don't want to upset you)
but there is a question I need you to
answer for me. I have an idea what your
answer is, but I'm not sure.

Last Tuesday, when we spent the evening together and had such a long talk, I got the feeling that you would be open to seeing me again. Was this the case, or were you just being nice?

I need to know so I can forget you if you don't want to see me.

If you want to see me, I would like to come to some understanding between us. (I don't need to go to bed with you, although I want that. I don't need to be the only guy in your life, although I'd like that. I don't need to see you a lot, although that would be wonderful. But I do need your Friendship (or to be able to forget you).)

I'm sorry if my caring about you has caused you pain. I never wanted that.

Darrell

I dressed and put my rain things on, folded the letter and put it in an envelope which I addressed to her. It was only about eight in the morning, and everybody else in my building was asleep or just getting up. I went downstairs. The rain wasn't bad, but I walked the couple of blocks to the bus stop in a hurry anyway—the sky was threatening. Fortunately there was a bus coming when I got to the stop. I got on and went right to the back. It was just me and the driver. The rain started up again. I almost missed her stop because I couldn't see out the window for all the rain. I got all the way up the hill to the front of her building, and then I had to stop and think about it. I had the letter in my hand, protected under my rain gear, and my hand was shaking. I thought about it. If I left her this letter, what would she think? She would think I was a fool, or too aggressive. I looked up at her windows. She couldn't be awake. Or maybe she hadn't come home at all. The thought struck me that she might be on her way home right now, though it was unlikely; but if she were, she might arrive, she might catch me standing in the rain like any ordinary fool, with my hand under my rain gear like some stupid Napoleon. This would never, ever do. I pulled the letter out and held it in front of me, and let the writing get wet and blurry, I wanted so badly to obliterate it right then. I crumpled the thing up and threw it in a trash can several doors down from her place.

I took the bus back to my neighborhood, where there was a bar I liked. I knew that it opened early in the mornings, because I'd spent some time there before. It was exactly what I needed, because it was dark and because nobody was going to ask me what I was doing there so early in the morning. It was my own feeling that early-morning drinking was nobody's business but the drinker's. I took the last booth, the one in the very back corner away from the bar, and I picked up the pieces of a newspaper from by the jukebox and I ordered whiskey with a beer chaser. It was the first of many that morning, which ended with my being very sick in the men's room. The bartender was concerned and asked if I wanted a cab when I came back out. I told him no, to just forget it, but he watched me. I ordered coffee, and he stopped. He must have decided I wasn't suicidal. So it was okay—I wasn't going to die in his stupid bar. I put on my rain things again after a while and went back out.

I stood under the awning for a while and watched the traffic and the rain coming down. I was fairly drunk. I didn't know what to do next. I couldn't concentrate on anything except Melissa. She was ruining my life. She wasn't telling me the truth. She must have sensed the connection between us. How could she ignore it? It was there. She is just like all the rest, ignoring the truth of the matter. The truth of the matter is that I am in love with her, and for some reason she is evasive about that fact, does not want to face it. This has happened to me before. There have been a number of other women. She is clearly not alone in this regard. Janet, Kathy, Susan, Marie, Karen. All of them were so evasive. They were all, oh so polite. Not one of them spoke the truth. I tried to be easy on them, tried not to ask too much of them. Is it so much to ask someone to love you back? Is it too much to ask someone to be close? That is all I want. A life with someone. A day to day life. All of those women showed me what they could be, showed me their kindness and their warmth, and then they just disappeared, turned away in one way or another when I came around. Oh, they would put on polite masks and talk the small talk, but when it came right down to it they weren't there for me, they couldn't face the truth of my love for them.

Somebody bumped my shoulder as he walked by me and into the bar. He looked at me but didn't say anything. That was good—I would have punched him if he had. I glared back at him, but by then he wasn't looking at me.

It was too cold and damp to stand out there anymore, so I turned up my collar and pulled my rain hat down low, and I went home.

I woke up Sunday dawn with a hangover. I couldn't remember anything after opening my front door Saturday afternoon. I was still wearing my rain things. I felt sick. I thought back and I realized that I hadn't eaten anything since Friday night. I hadn't missed eating, hadn't noticed.

I got up from my bed and took off my slicker and put it away, and I got out of my clothes and into the shower. The shower helped. It was raining very hard still as I dressed, so I decided not to go out. I fixed coffee and toast and eggs for breakfast, just the sort of breakfast I thought she might have on a rainy Sunday. I pulled some photos of her out of my desk drawer and went through them while I ate. She didn't know that I had been photographing her around school. I had taken color photos mostly, so I could remember everything about her in color, even though it meant sending the pictures out for processing and was expensive. There were always other people in the pictures, too, since I couldn't get her alone and take her picture without her knowing it. This wasn't satisfactory, but it had to do. I propped all the pictures up in a row on my desk where I could see them at a glance.

The rain kept up, so there was no going out. I spent part of the day writing poems and letters to Melissa and tearing each one up because it wasn't good enough. I spent some time with my photos, a ruler and a grease pencil, trying find ways of cropping the pictures to maximize her image and to cut out the others around her. I made a mental note to get a book on color processing.

I'll tell you something about women. The more you love them, the more uppity they get. They begin to act like dictators. I drew a little grease-pencil Hitler mustache on Melissa's face and quickly wiped it off.

Thank God it wasn't raining Monday. I could feel the beginnings of a cold coming on. I slept in a little bit, knowing she had an afternoon class and I'd probably find her there. I left my place at about eleven and walked down to Colorado Boulevard, turned left, and walked toward school. I stopped at the one shop that really interested me, an old pawn shop. They had some good things, nice old knives with interesting carved handles, old guns, things like that. Stuff that didn't sell.

I stopped at a Winchell's and got a couple of donuts and coffee to go and walked the rest of the way to school. I went up the front walk where the pools are, but I didn't see her. So, I went by the photo lab and sat there until I'd finished the coffee and donuts, did a couple of small chores, then decided to look for her again. I went out the front entrance of the main building, which has a long flight of stairs and from where you can see who is in the pool area. I had a hunch Melissa might be there. Sure enough, there she was on a bench by one of the pools. I sat down on the stairs so I would be less conspicuous. I got to watch her for a while anyway before she saw me. She was wearing new boots, red, her favorite color. I realized that I was really getting to know her, all those little preferences and habits, even down to new additions to her wardrobe. She saw me after a little bit, but she didn't leave. Then the person sitting next to her left, and there was a place for me. I hurried over there before someone else could take my place.

I stopped in front of her. Her eyes were closed; she had her head tilted back a little bit. I could have leaned over and kissed her so easily. She didn't open her eyes until I spoke. She didn't seem startled. I had a seat.

It wasn't right, though. She didn't even try to carry on a conversation with me. She wouldn't look at me. It made me angry. I let her know I knew she was avoiding me. I told her that right off the bat. She made stupid, cruel excuses, as though being "busy" was an excuse to ignore another

human being. Especially considering what we'd begun together, how she had acted like she cared about me as a
person. I poured my heart out to her. I told her how I
suffered over her avoiding me. She said the most absurd
things, asked if I had a *girlfriend*. What did she think this
was all about? She said we hardly knew each other!

I offered her time. I told her I could be patient, let us
have time to work on it. Then she admitted it. There was
someone else in her life.

That got to me, got me right where it hurts. I was willing
to compromise. I offered her that. She wasn't really listening to me. She was looking away. It seemed she was about
to stand up and go. She began to move as though she would
stand, and I did something that shocked me; I grabbed her
arm and held on. That got her attention. She glared at me
and I let go, shocked at the way she looked at me. I was
certain she would never speak to me again, so I left as
quickly as I could, trying not to be conspicuous.

That was it. I went right home. I packed an overnight
bag and got a heavy jacket. I locked up my place and
walked down to Colorado Boulevard, climbed on a bus
and rode to the freeway on-ramp near Orange Grove,
north-bound. My mind was like a stupid double exposure, with Melissa superimposed on the freeway image. I
stuck my thumb out and waited. She was a jinx. She had
a boyfriend. She was busy. The jacket was too warm, so I
took it off and set it on the overnight bag between my
feet. I waited with my thumb sticking out. Cars went by.
I could feel their wind. Stupid bitch. A *girlfriend*.

A guy in a trailer-truck stopped for me. He said he was
headed for Oregon. I pushed my bag in and threw my coat

on top, pulled myself into the cab. This was the first time I had been in a big truck like that. The driver could see I was interested and he explained it to me, about the gears and the tonnage it could haul, and the bunks behind the seat where two could sleep on a long trip. He said he was hauling TVs, electronic equipment. He told me he had recently come off a cross-country trip—straight shot across Interstate 80, he said—and he told me how he had used his CB radio to keep track of the highway patrol so he wouldn't get speeding tickets. He said they all had those little radios, and every now and then they would check in with each other to give the locations of the cops. That sounded okay to me. It sounded like an okay life.

After a while he turned the radio on and tuned to a country-western station. I pulled my jacket over me and went to sleep. I woke up when the truck pulled into a weigh station near Bakersfield. The driver looked over and said he would be driving all night and did I want to come along for the ride? That set me off again thinking. When I didn't answer him right away he asked where I was going, and I said "San Francisco." It just popped out of my mouth. I hadn't ever been there before. It seemed as good a place as any. I wished I had brought my camera.

Well, we didn't get into San Francisco until about ten o'clock at night, and he dropped me off near the shipyards because he wasn't going through town. It was awfully cold, even with my jacket. The driver had said that there were some hotels nearby. I checked into the first one I found, an old brick building under the freeway with an old man at the desk. The place had a bar right next door, so after putting my bag in my room I went back downstairs for a drink. It was all old guys and dockworkers in there, and no women. That was fine with me. I got drunk on boilermakers and I didn't get sick. Nobody paid attention to me. A couple of guys were playing pool and everybody was watching them. They had a nice old Wurlitzer in there, the kind with multicolored lights and bubbles running through the tubes. Somebody played that Rolling Stones song "Angie" about a dozen times. Probably somebody's girlfriend was named Angie.

Next day I checked out and did some walking. I thought about taking a ferry somewhere, since I was right there near the ferry building, but I didn't know any of those places. I walked down Market Street instead. I didn't like it much. I rode a cable car. It took me into a better neighborhood, up on a hill. I went into one of those hotels, all the way to the bar at the top. Drunk in the morning again. It occurred to me that I hadn't brought enough money to stay in San Francisco very long. I counted my money. It was certainly colder here than I would have thought. I went to the lounge and called a couple of the airlines. I had enough to fly home, that was about it. There was an airport bus that could take me right from this hotel. That's what I did.

It was hot in Los Angeles, and very sunny. It took a while to figure out just how to get out of the airport. There was a bus to the Sheraton in Pasadena. From there it was a cab ride back to my place, after a drink. The people at the hotel were polite, even though I was obviously just passing through. At my place I had a shower and changed. I got my camera and went to school. Everybody was hanging around outside. Warm weather out of season makes everyone so stupid, as if a holiday had been declared, or a general strike. All the political stuff seemed to happen in good weather. It wasn't real.

I went across the quad, keeping an eye out for her. It took time to sort through all the faces on the way with everybody milling around and people stretched out in odd places getting sun. There are ledges around the planters and if people lie down by those ledges you can't always see them. And she likes the sun. I had in mind a picture or two if nobody noticed.

I couldn't find her, so I sat by the library and did some architectural shots, trying to work in some interesting patches of sky. I could almost smell her. If I closed my eyes and sat still, I could imagine smelling her hair.

She was there that evening, in the darkroom, busy as could be. I held off, let her work, but I kept an eye on her just the same. Once burned. This was a test. She could be a cunt or make things right. That simple. I gave her one last chance to make what she would of it; she asked a question about the darkroom and I answered it. It was clear enough that she hadn't noticed me before I spoke, and her reaction wasn't favorable. Her vanity took over, and she hurried off. Pretense, all pretense. I watched her just to let her know I knew. I had her at last, stripped to the bone. The truth about Melissa.

She tried to pull that trick again, about leaving when I wasn't looking. But I was looking this time and I followed her, all the way to her car. It would have been easy enough to slip up behind her. Naturally, I didn't.

I got her the next day though. I caught her in the hall, put her up against the wall and held her there with both hands. No more lies. I asked her why she wouldn't talk to me. It worked. She agreed to talk to me right then. We went back to the scene of our first real talk—her apartment.

I laid out the possibilities. I explained that I knew she was seeing someone else, which would be a legitimate reason for her not seeing me as often as I would like. But we could have a more or less platonic relationship for now. We wouldn't necessarily have to be lovers.

She tried to interrupt me once, probably to give me that crap about moving things along too fast, so I set her straight on a couple of points. I told her about those other girls I'd been involved with, and how she wasn't as important as her vanity would have her think. She wasn't the best one I'd known. She wasn't perfect, by any means. But the greatest possibilities for a romantic and even physical relationship were with her.

She told me that she couldn't have any relationship with me whatsoever. She mentioned "responsibility." She said our first conversation was an "accident." It was all lies.

I cut the conversation short, just got up and left her there talking to herself.

✳

You know, that argument didn't upset me so much. I don't mind so much that she doesn't want to see me. But I am angry about her reasons and her attitude toward what happened between us. I resent her feeling that everything is my fault. She's either not being realistic or she's being damn unfair. I had thought she might be less vain than that.

During the argument she mentioned that "accidental" until 4 a.m. conversation we had in January. She seemed to think that event was largely or entirely responsible for my present feelings for her. That is not so. Admittedly, I became very interested in her because of that conversation, but that interest was not the high point of my feelings for her and there were other times that we talked. I did not attribute any special feelings toward me on her part because she talked to me, outside of a possible mild interest. How presumptuous of me!

The days right after the argument were bad. She had been pretty hard on me. Although I realized that part of her venom towards the end of that argument was caused by my unintentional stab at her vanity, she certainly achieved her objective. I was going to avoid her as much as possible. On the first day I busted up my apartment, starting with the mirror in the bathroom. I was sure she thought I was repulsive. I went back to my old haunts and got drunk and stayed drunk for several days.

I really didn't think that my absence would be noticed, especially by her. You can't imagine my shock at returning to hear from my landlady that Melissa had worried about my abrupt disappearance. I had thought her intent during that argument was to finalize things between us. I thought that was what she wanted, and I felt it was the best thing for me, because I found being around her a bit stressful. I was puzzled that she was making no effort to end things between us. Rather, she had gone to great effort to look me up! I began wondering if we might be friends. Only friends, I *never* had any idea that she wanted me romantically or even physically. Is it really so wild for me to have thought that she might be agreeable to a more or less platonic relationship? I'm not blind to the fact that there are problems in maintaining a more or less platonic relationship when one party (me) cares about the other party romantically and physically. I know that, even if she cares about me as a person, there are several legitimate reasons for her not wanting to see me, like—her feeling uncomfortable around me, her feeling that seeing me would not be in my best interest, her feeling that my presence might mess up something she has going with someone else, et cetera. These reasons I could understand and accept, and she would already have heard the last from me.

But if she feels that she can't see me because she never wanted anything to do with me; that because of a socio- or psycho-disorder, I misinterpreted her intent when she first spoke with me, thinking she had an interest in me; and acting on this misinterpretation, I forced myself on her—I find this reason illegitimate, inaccurate and extremely cruel. I might understand how she could feel this way if I had put a lot of pressure on her to change her mind about me, but I don't honestly feel that I ever put much pressure on her. Of all the girls I've been interested in, she's the one I put the least pressure on, yet she should be able to handle pressure better than any of the rest. It's bad enough to have someone I love tell me that she won't or can't see me without her falsely thinking I'm ill because I love her.

I appreciate her concern in looking for me after the argument. She can't know how appreciative I am for that. She is a much kinder person than her vanity would want to accept.

I'm sorry for all the irritation I caused her. I doubt if she knows how much I wish things had turned out different—or why—but I know it's not the end of the world.

I won't annoy her again—that's my promise to her. Unless she further provokes me.